Death in Sils Maria

Ulrich Knellwolf

ISBN 978-0-9955093-3-7

The book was first published in German under the title
Tod in Sils Maria in 2009.

This edition is a translation by Iris Hunter, Cambridge

The copyright of the cover photograph belongs to
Gian Giovanoli

Cover design by Duncan Bamford,
Insight Illustration Ltd
http://www.insightillustration.co.uk/

Copyediting by Jan Andersen
Creativecopywriter.org

Republished in English by:

PERFECT PUBLISHERS LTD
23 Maitland Avenue
Cambridge
CB4 1TA
England
http://www.perfectpublishers.co.uk

About the author

Ulrich Knellwolf, born in 1942, grew up in the German part of Switzerland. After studying theology in Basel, Bonn and Zurich, he graduated with a doctorate on the 19th-century Swiss author and priest Jeremias Gotthelf, who also combined narrative and theology.

Knellwolf has been a priest since 1969 and published the first of many books in 1992. He is not only an acclaimed author of many short stories and novels, but has also written influential academic essays, treatises and books in the field of theology.

He is much respected and has won many significant awards for his work.

Author's preface to the English translation

Tod in Sils Maria comprising 'thirteen wicked tales' was first published in 1993; eleven years later, the original thirteen became seventeen — there is, after all, no lack of sinister stories in the world.

Fifteen years later still, these tales should feel honoured to appear in English and I am grateful to Iris Hunter for her translation. I hope that she and I will have many readers who will enjoy the stories.

* * * * * * * * * * *

A wealthy Englishman is taken to a lonely ski track and disappears in the silently falling snow. . . A shot reverberates through the comfortable foyer of a luxury hotel during late afternoon: a secret has been discovered and revenge was the only plausible option . . . Heavily wrapped up figures with goggles seem to push cross-country skiers from the trail — is it possible that sportsmen can vanish without a trace?

Suspense is the essential ingredient. The goings-on are described chillingly but always with a wicked sense of dark humour. The contrasts between the sun-drenched mountains where tourists enjoy their winter sports and the elegant dinners where expensive wines are consumed by candlelight are very evocative. Will the graceful skier get down without a ghastly accident? Has someone poisoned that guest's glass of exquisite wine?

Contents

End of February

In the morning there will be continuing high pressure outdoors as well as indoors.

'The weather conditions are extremely stable', smiled Renato, the concierge.

The author felt as if he was in paradise, left the hotel, looked at the peaks, rubbed his hands and set out for the Fextal. Past the Chesa Oscar, he turned to the right, away from the path and into a light wood. Not a soul could be seen; the world was his. Further on, the sun burnt his forehead and a few solitary cross-country skiers could be seen in the distance. Had he not feared that they would interpret it as a cry for help, he would have shouted for joy.

Soon afterwards, the path became steep. He broke out in a sweat and started panting and, as always at this spot, he had to rest for a while. Normally, he did not mind, but today he did: high above him, somebody — propped up on his hiking stick — looked down on him. It seemed as if he was laughing to himself about the chap down there, who was clearly out of breath.

'Toff!' the author thought, 'don't be so smug. This is my valley and it's none of your business whether I run or stand still!'

He lowered his head, trudged on and refused to raise his eyes again. When he arrived at the top, the annoying observer had already disappeared.

Not long thereafter, he saw him again, barely thirty, forty steps ahead of him.

'Ha', he thought, 'I'll be dashing past you and you will stop laughing.'

The bloke was thin and tall, carried his stick horizontally like the pole of a tightrope walker, and pulled up his knees like a stork.

'Look at these shoes! People never learn. In this season you cannot even make it from Sils Maria to Baselgia with shoes like that. Light brown loafers, probably Italian, possibly even with leather soles. As for the rest of his appearance! Presumably tweed and a maroon scarf wrapped around his neck like the boa of a cabaret dancer.'

The man turned to the left, before the author managed to overtake him.

'Typical that he had taken a forbidden shortcut. Light blue tracks are only for cross-country skiers. He'll destroy their freshly prepared loipe, but types like him could not care less.'

He kept to the red posts and followed them towards the right. Another ascent. On the summit, there were two old friends, he bare-chested, she in a skimpy top and with skin like leather, not a pretty sight, and they were in the process of tanning themselves further. He decided not to be the first to greet them; they had no doubt thought along the same lines.

Having crossed the patch of forest above, he reached the highest point. The bench was unoccupied and he sat down for a while, but only opened the zip of his jacket. Below him the stork with the balancing pole appeared. He pranced as if the dazzlingly white snow were in fact muddy sludge. The author grinned about so much unworldliness.

The author's path led past the Zellweger farm. It was lunch time and the young farmer was on the balcony. They knew each other; he waved and the farmer returned the gesture.

'No ski school?'

'No, not today.'

Further up there were building works. The red signpost showed the way to the Pensiun Crasta. There was no way around it; the thought was mouth-watering. Ragout of ibex, with wine from the Valtellina and, to finish it off, blueberry cake. He had to have this meal at least once during his annual holidays in February; this year it was clearly due early, on the second day already.

The first door in the dark corridor led to the kitchen. He knocked and opened. Frau Padrun stood in the midst of steam and hissing pots, emerged from the clouds like the angel, and shook his hand. He sat down at the only available table. The serious-looking Italian waitress had been here for years.

'We do have ibex again', she said, as she handed over the menu. 'And a half of Valtellina, as usual?'

The first bite tasted wonderful. He was just about to have the second mouthful, when bleating emerged from a sort of alcove behind his back complaining like a goat: 'Do you think I could pay now, Miss?'

He recognised the voice. He had heard it during a telephone conversation and, with the first word, it transformed his paradise to a school room, where grades were handed out pitilessly. The aptly named Müller-Schwartenmagen.[1] This chap had written such a ghastly review, a mixture of disgust and self-pity, of his penultimate book, that the author felt reduced to a snail; the piece would not have been more horrible if the author's work had been the critic's under-age sister and the author had sexually abused her. The critic did not even acknowledge the author's last novel anymore. The author had taken revenge through a letter to the editor about an article the critic had written on Gotthelf, in which he accused him of sheer ignorance.

'A mineral water and an espresso', he heard the Italian waitress repeat. Shortly thereafter, the critic walked past him and left. It was him — the chap with the light-brown leather soles, the maroon scarf and the walking stick. He cast disgusted glances left and right. One touched the author who, like a lurking dog, squinted at him from below. Müller-Schwartenmagen walked past him with a completely straight face: he did not recognise the author.

The ibex suddenly tasted of nothing; the Valtellina was corked. The author had lost his appetite. He waited for ten minutes, expecting the critic to have gone past the Restaurant Sonne already, despite his inadequate footwear.

'No espresso?' The Italian waitress was amazed.

The author departed without saying goodbye to the kitchen staff. He took the path to Platta below the 'Sonne'. The other one would not have dared go down there. The author wanted

---

[1] Schwartenmagen means 'brawn' in German.

to avoid meeting him again and hoped he had only come up for a day excursion. He blamed himself for reacting in such an exaggerated way. At the same time, he knew that the wall of his paradise had started to crack.

Renato, the concierge, was surprised at his early return when he handed him the key.

It turned out impossible to continue with work on his novel: the voice of the goat gave a vitriolic running commentary to every sentence he wrote. He might as well have written the review himself — on a separate piece of paper. He suffered. At seven o'clock he took a bath and then got dressed. He liked looking decent for dinner and despised people who turned up in a jumper and jeans.

He had occupied the same table for years. This time with pleasant neighbours, as he had noted with satisfaction the day before, but the old lady must have departed earlier in the day. Her place was now taken by a figure who was obviously aggrieved by the world in general, the hotel, the trivial people around him, by the food and particularly by the book that lay open next to his plate: Müller-Schwartenmagen. At least the author did not have to sit in his visual horizon. The critic, however, could not avoid sitting in the author's field of vision and his meal was thus ruined. Mind you, he seemed not to enjoy his soup either — he left most of it. And the book, too, clearly ruined his appetite. He fingered it in between courses, as if the pages were infected.

'It could be my book', the author thought darkly. Out of sheer desperation he finished a whole bottle. When he left the dining room before dessert — observed with indifference by the critic — he had to be hellishly careful not to sway.

The Trio had just begun its usual evening concert. He nodded in the direction of the cellist in a chummy fashion; years ago he had played a solo suite by Bach at one of his readings. Here, too, he had his fixed seat where he drank his espresso and his grappa, usually followed by a wheat beer in a thick tall tumbler. There was a card on the little table.

'Isn't it nice that Rodney made a reservation for me', he thought to himself and sat down. Instead of asking what he wanted — he knew, after all, what it was — he flapped his arms like a wounded bird.

'So sorry', he whispered.

The author grabbed the card, which read 'Dr Müller-Schwartenmagen'.

A picture of fury, dejection and despair, he got up, leaving Rodney in a state of bewilderment, and went out, took the lift upstairs and drank half a bottle of scotch from the fridge in the room. Had he found Müller-Schwartenmagen sprawled over his armchair or sleeping in his bed, he would not have been surprised.

What to do? This was his place. He would not give it up without a fight. Not to the critic.

26 February

He slept amazingly well, nevertheless. Not surprising after all the wine and schnapps. When the author came down, the other one was already at breakfast, of course. And again, the unspeakable maroon scarf was wrapped around his neck.

6

He read the *Frankfurter Allgemeine*, which seemed to cause him stomach ache, and he hardly ate. The author choked on a roll: he was in a hurry and clearly in a bad mood.

'Your espresso will be here in a minute', Francisco told him, as he had done for years.

'Not today', he responded; the Portuguese was totally confused.

In the foyer he leant towards Renato across the counter in a conspiratorial way and said: 'Müller-Schwartenmagen. How long is he staying?'

Renato leafed through a book. Then he exclaimed, smiling in the belief that the information would cheer up the author: 'To the day as long as you are!'

The author was devastated. Should he leave? But surely not to escape from this chap!

'People like him don't dare to go on the lake', he thought and walked across the ice to Isola. Who sat in the pub there, with a face as if he had devoured a plate of horseshoe nails, poisoning his surroundings with his looks? And who, please, made straight for the 'Edelweiss', where the author, as usual, wanted to drink an afternoon gin and tonic? And he always carried a book under his arm, just like a hangman dragging a delinquent to the gallows. Gallows was the correct term. The author would judge him. For once, the author would be the judge and the critic would be the accused. And he would be just as merciless in his judgement over the critic as he was over him.

During a restless night, the author imagined all sorts of possible manners of death. Someone who disturbed the peace of his little world must be prepared for the worst. He had, after all, made it for himself fairly and honestly, literally acquiring it with his stories. He read to an extremely large audience up here every year. He had been invited to deliver the official speech on 1 August, the Swiss national holiday. Not even Müller-Schwartenmagen could take this from him. Either the critic disappeared of his own account or he would help him on his way.

He needed time to think; no excursion to the Fextal today, nor to Isola, but a trip with the postbus to Maloja, and from there on foot towards Lake Cavloccia. After half an hour, Müller-Schwartenmagen came towards him, balancing his walking stick.

'It looks almost as if he were doing target practice, as one would with a rifle.'

They crossed paths. The author was reminded of Schiller's Gessler and William Tell. He muttered a greeting into the collar of his jacket; the critic was blind, deaf and mute.

'What's this?' the author thought as he continued his walk. 'You trek into the Fextal; the critic is there. You walk over the lake to Isola; the critic sits there, too. You try to evade him by taking the path towards Lake Cavloccia; the critic walks towards you. He is always there before you, as if your echo spoke first, as if your shadow was overtaking you. Does he read my thoughts? Is he ambushing me? High time to defend myself!'

Müller-Schwartenmagen did not show any inclination to shorten his stay. This would have been surprising, given the lovely weather. The snow had already become a bit slushy on the mountain sides exposed to the sun and that gave the author an idea.

It was not a matter of revenge. This place was at stake: he was not willing to have it contested by the schoolmaster, judge of the arts, hawk of exam marks, hangman of creativity. Both of them could not be peacefully in this place together. Either the author or the critic. Incompatibility of blood group, rhesus factor, poisoning, rejection. He was not the sheep that could be led to the slaughterhouse.

The snow would help, the sun would help, and Müller-Schwartenmagen himself would also help. For the first time, the critic would help, namely by getting rid of the critic. The snow helped, because a lot of it had fallen before these beautiful sunny days had started. The sun helped, because it had warmed up the snow a lot, nearly boiled it soft, so to speak, i.e. considerable risk of avalanches. And Müller-Schwartenmagen helped, because he was a classic, bolshy and stubborn teacher, who focused exclusively on exams and grades — one who never left the classroom.

'He has nothing else in his head but following me, my silent echo, the shadow that precedes me. I tempt the idiot — such a pedant when it comes to marking schoolbooks — and clearly a fool who has never left the classroom, further back into the Fextal. There, in the sunny western mountainside, the snow turns slippery like soap. I'll eat my hat if I cannot lie in wait for him further above and trigger an avalanche. Why else have I been in the mountain infantry, after all? It has been a long time, but you never lose the eye for the conditions and how easy it is to bring movement into a mass of snow. If you want to avoid avalanches, you must be able to cause them. Merely a small avalanche, but big enough to swallow one Müller-Schwartenmagen. Tomorrow, Sir, I shall take the cable car to the Corvatsch and ski from there to the Fextal. We'll see whether, there too, you will be coming towards me!'

Today, the author only went into the village and hired skis and boots. Out of the corner of his eye, he saw the critic buy something he could pull over his light brown shoes to stop him slipping. Later on, during lunch, he observed with pity the tweed-covered back and the hand that fingered the printed pages, as if they were infectious.

29 February

On the sun terrace of the Hotel Fex, the publisher held binoculars to his eyes, having taken off his fur jacket and opened the top three buttons of his shirt. Next to him, fur coat over her shoulders, sat his lady friend Angéline, who could have been his granddaughter.

'There he is', the publisher said quietly. 'I really think it's him. What a sight: my author on skis. And over there Müller-Schwartenmagen. Nobody would have predicted at his cradle that he would one day go on stalking tours in the Fextal.'

He put his binoculars down and turned to the mixed sherbet. 'Now we only have to wait.'

'But not for too long', moaned Angéline. 'You promised to drive me to St Moritz before the shops close.'

'Not to worry; this won't take long.'

'Is there no risk of avalanches on that slope?'

'Quite. That's the point.'

'You don't like those two, do you? Why don't you?'

'Müller-Schwartenmagen is a pompous ass who does not get off his high horse, not even for a first-class meal. He has ruined my business for the whole last season with his scribbling. The other, well, is slowly becoming a burden for my balance sheet. No more ideas, language and expression gone — nothing.'

'Could one call this waste management?' Angéline whispered.

'Clever girl! In some sense one could, indeed, call it waste disposal.'

'You bribed Renato!'

'That was not difficult. An old acquaintance. He sounded out our Mr Author a bit, planted the information with the critic very discreetly and all was well.'

He picked up his binoculars again and said: 'He has seen him now.'

'Who has seen and who has been seen?'
'The author has seen the critic. Comes to a halt and hops around on his skis in a slightly weird way, clearly trying to

cause an avalanche. There! Müller-Schwartenmagen looks up. Recognises him and raises his walking stick to his shoulder like a rifle.'

'What does he want with this?'

'To shoot, of course. This walking stick, my dear girl, is a gun. An antique. In the nineteenth century they produced walking sticks with the most unusual inner workings. Take aim nicely. Shoot!'

'Not so loudly!'

'Hit! And what have I predicted? An avalanche has been triggered. Müller-Schwartenmagen turns back. He has no chance.'

Satisfied, the publisher packs his binoculars into their case.

'Waitress, the bill, please! And please tell the driver to get the car ready.'

'The one from the Suvretta?'

'Yes, of course. Hurry up, Angéline. What are you waiting for?'

Story writing competition

The Sils competition for the best story was to end with the prize giving in the summer. Our jury of seven had had five long meetings to choose a shortlist of ten from among the surprising abundance of entries; three would win a prize and the other seven would be published, as would the prize winners' stories. The tourist office invited all authors and their partners to a festive event in the church of Sils Maria, followed by dinner, as well as an overnight stay.

The celebration proceeded smoothly. Everyone was happy, except for one author, who ran out of the church in the middle of the ceremony never to be seen again. Puzzling over possible reasons for this was the topic of most dinner conversations. The unanimous view was that she had probably been disappointed not to have been one of the three prize winners. Apart from that, there were no feelings of envy, nor of schadenfreude. In the final session of the jury we had been slightly sceptical and astonished to notice that two of the seven stories selected were by the same author, but that was not against the rules. Neither of them made the top three. Unfortunately, the author, with the rather striking name of A.M. Brosbier, stayed away from the prize-giving ceremony, without explanation. I was all the more curious about him when it emerged that, according to the secretary of the jury, he had submitted not only two, but a total of seventeen stories. One of us added laughingly: 'Who knows, he may be the author of all stories.'

Except for these little irritations, it was a fine event and everyone was pleased. It transpired that most of the authors had attended a creative writing course in the Upper Engadin and were regular holidaymakers in the region. The longer the evening lasted, the more we liked each other, and we ended up agreeing to meet again on the Wednesday of the second week in February, same time, same place.

Back home, I searched the internet for Brosbier, the author of the seventeen stories, but without success. No man with this name lived in Switzerland or anywhere else — or he did not have a telephone. At least I had his address, a street and house number in a small village near Zurich. The administrative offices of the alleged town confirmed that the street that was mentioned existed, though not the number, and that the citizen in question was completely unknown. Someone had played a practical joke on us — if a harmless one. Even so, my thoughts went to Brosbier every now and then, the mysterious storyteller.

Toni got in touch with me in the autumn. Toni was a teacher, around fifty, wrote stories in his spare time, worked on a novel and intended to give up school and try out the life of a freelance writer — his dream for as long as he could remember, as he had told me over dinner in Sils. His story 'Light is truth' had won third prize in the competition: he asked if he could visit me and, as it sounded urgent, I met him the next day.

Toni was deeply worried. As soon as the little book with the Sils stories had been published, he had received a letter from Ambrose Bierce, in which the sender claimed that Toni had stolen the prize-winning story from him; he also said he had proof and would bring an action.

'Bierce? Someone is trying to pull our leg', I said. 'Is he after money?'

'No.'

'That will be next.'

'I do not believe so', said Toni. 'The letter was, after all, sent two months ago, and no financial demand has arrived yet.'

'So you don't have to worry anymore.'

That was not how he saw it, Toni countered. Indeed, since the first letter, he was being bombarded with more letters almost daily, with increasingly absurd demands.

'According to the latest, I am supposed to take out a full-page ad in the *Neue Zürcher Zeitung* admitting that my story is a copy of Bierce's.'

'Unpleasant, these nutters. Nevertheless, forget it. The real Ambrose Bierce has been dead for nearly 90 years.'

'That, precisely, is far from clear. In 1913, he went to Mexico, during the Civil War, when he was 71. Since then, nothing has been heard of him. His body was never found and there are at least half a dozen theories about how, when and where he died.'

'Most importantly: he died. Surely, you don't believe. . . ?'

He did not believe, and yet. What did the French noble woman of the 18th century say? 'I don't believe in ghosts, but I fear them.' Toni was afraid.

'What could he do to you?'

'If he accuses me of plagiarism, I am finished. It's nearly impossible to prove the opposite. And he seems to have evidence.'

15

Toni pulled out a small volume. 'Evil stories' by Ambrose Bierce.

'Here.' He opened the book and put it in front of him.

The story's title was 'Light and truth' and if it was by Bierce, then Toni had indeed mostly copied it.

'He sent me this book. The bizarre thing is that I found it in two second-hand booksellers. Without this story, though.'

'Torn out?'

'No. No gap. Not part of it.'

What should I advise? It would be nonsensical to consult a lawyer, as nonsensical as consulting a psychiatrist. So I said: 'Put cotton buds in your ears and finish your novel.'

'He accuses me of stealing that as well.'

'In that case more cotton buds. And don't open any more letters!'

He thanked me and left, but I noticed, when I observed him walking away, that I had not been a great help. I heard nothing else from him. Until winter.

Three weeks before the agreed meeting in Sils, a death notice appeared in the newspaper. He must have died in an accident. I could not go to the service, because I had to do a reading in the Romandie on the same day. I wrote a few lines to his widow and received a pre-printed card of thanks in response.

We met in the Chesa Pool and I noticed at once that they were all afraid. I heard that Toni had died in a car crash; he had not been at fault, but the other driver, who had caused the accident, had fled the scene and had so far not been recognised.

'He had received threatening letters', said one author.

I tried to calm everyone, but noticed that I was not up-to-date with events. They had all received threatening letters and were still getting them. Some before Toni's death, others since then and very recently, letters from Ambrose Bierce, in which he demanded an official admission that he was the author of their stories.

'Toni had not reacted. And now he is dead.'

Wakes are normally jolly affairs, which tend to get merrier with time. Our meal was full of unrelenting mourning and grief. Nobody had an appetite; the kitchen was no doubt in a state of deep depression. When everything was cleared away, we sat like a group of alcoholics around the table, held onto our glasses and were silent, and the longer we were silent, the more difficult it became to say something. At last, someone muttered: 'Let's go to bed.'

Most slept in the hotel overnight — if they were able to sleep, that is. Nobody was properly awake in the morning. Then Isolde ran downstairs screeching.

'He was here! I have seen him!'

'Who?'

'Meier!'

'Meier?'

'The one whose creative writing course we attended. He was lurking around the house.'

We ran outside. Perhaps we had the wrong Bierce. We found nobody, neither Meier nor Bierce.

'What did he look like, your Meier?' I asked, when we sat at the table again. Veronika had a picture. The group of well-known faces and, right in the centre, would you believe it, with curly ginger hair, a ginger moustache, as I knew him from portraits . . .

'Bierce', I stuttered.

'No, Meier', Veronika contradicted.

'No, Bierce', I said. 'Perhaps he was already here in the summer. And perhaps that lady who ran out of the church in a mad rush had recognised him.'

They looked at me in horror.

I should add two things: Isolde, who had won second prize in the competition and wanted to stay on for a week's skiing in the Fextal, died in an unexplained accident on the third day, when she and another skier ran into each other on Corvatsch. The other skier could not be found. As for me, when I got home, I found a letter in the post referring to my two volumes of stories. I have been slightly worried ever since then.

A modest proposal[2]

The hotel prided itself on being very child-friendly. Because discounts for the little ones were substantial, many people arrived with their offspring. Sometimes Regula and Rolf felt disturbed by the children, particularly at breakfast and dinner. The screaming was reminiscent of a crèche. There was the option of an early dinner for the kids under the supervision of a nursery nurse, but few parents used this service. Most preferred to take their youngsters to the dining room, where they created havoc, exhausted from ski school, but still overwrought.

Regula and Rolf were childless, and bringing up children was therefore pure theory to them. But in their view, most parents spoilt their kids massively and set no limits.

'If my child made such a racket, I would take him out at once', said Regula.

'And out there I would smack his bottom', added Rolf.

Because of the children, they used to go to breakfast early and to dinner late. The kids, and their parents, were not up before nine o'clock, and in the evening most were in bed just after nine. By being careful about the timing, their meals were hardly disturbed, and during the day the youngsters were obviously not in the hotel. This year, furthermore, there appeared to be no children living in the rooms to the right and left of theirs, nor above and below — in any case, they heard nothing.

---

[2] The heading in the original German is 'Bündnerfleisch', a regional specialty of dry-cured meat, for which the canton of Grisons is famous.

19

Rolf was very glad about that, as he was intent on writing for three hours every day. Nowhere else could he work as well as here.

'The right climate for the brain!' he said.

They got up at eight and were at breakfast shortly before nine. They ate heartily, as this had to last until dinner time. When the noisy families arrived, Regula and Rolf were already in the lobby, looking through the day's post and reading the two papers, which they had had forwarded to them from home. And by the time the kids were full and ran through the lobby, the two of them were already in the lift on the way up to change for the daily walk. They left the hotel between eleven and twelve.

They normally chose one of two paths: one day the one, the next the other. The first led them through the forest down to the lake and then across the ice, and, depending on how fit they felt, on to Isola or all the way to Maloja. The second track was a fairly steep climb to the Fextal, to Crasta, from there down to Platta, past the Chesa Pool to the ravine and through it into the village. On this second path, they always passed a farm with a porch where a dozen or so big, long pieces of meat were hanging to dry.

'On the last day we'll go past here again and buy a couple of pounds of Bündnerfleisch. Dry-cured in the fresh air, as this is, will taste particularly good', Regula remarked each time.

Shortly after two they were back. Regula had a lie-down and slept for a long time; Rolf fell asleep, too, snoozed until three o'clock, and then sat down with his laptop to write. One more big book, perhaps his most important — saving Jonathan Swift's honour theologically. As is well known,

Swift was an Anglican priest in the Church of Ireland, who would have loved to become a bishop, but only managed to be promoted to Dean of St Patrick's Cathedral in Dublin. Apart from *Gulliver's Travels*, he published bitter pamphlets and vicious satires and, to this day, theologians are so embarrassed that they give him a wide berth. Rolf, on the other hand, had always held him in high esteem as an original theologian. Now he wanted to prove his thesis and make the world of divinity aware of what they were missing by ignoring Swift's scholarship.

'You really think it's worth it?' his friend Feierabend, who was teaching systematic theology at a German university, had asked. 'Admittedly, I know only his sermon about being asleep in church, apart from *Gulliver*, of course, which I read as a child. Theologically pretty feeble, I have to say. And then there is, you know, the — err — "Modest Proposal", this satire about . . . you know what.'

'The impoverished Irish fattening their own children and selling their flesh as a tasty delicacy to the wealthy English', Rolf had added, completing the sentence.

'Gruesome!'

'Don't forget that the author was a theologian.'

'What is this supposed to mean?' Feierabend asked outraged.

'Is human sacrifice not a biblical topic?'

'Not the most fundamental one, I'd say.'

'Not so sure about that', countered Rolf.
'As long as you don't break your teeth on the old cannibal.'

21

Rolf had responded with a laugh: 'Human flesh is supposed to be tender, even that of the elderly.'

He did not tell Regula that he had just started with the sensitive chapter about the 'Modest Proposal'. She would have had great qualms, even bigger than Feierabend's. Each book renewed her concern for Rolf's reputation, but while Feierabend was prone to academic opportunism, completely internalised in his case, it was a matter of love for Regula. She wanted to prevent Rolf from slicing into his own flesh, which would make him something of a self-eater, as he thought to himself with a smile.

The chapter about the 'Modest Proposal' should have a central position in the book. It would bring together the thoughts of the whole. The first part related to Swift's disguise theology, based upon his study of the Second Epistle to the Corinthians. Here, Rolf believed he had discovered highly unusual, not to say disconcerting, connections to St Paul. Thus, he expressed, as a summary of this part, the hypothesis that Swift the theologian had taken the Pauline metaphors literally in a surreal way.

The second part was about Swift's scatological language, which — surprisingly — linked him to Luther and might suggest that they were rather close in other respects, too.

The third part of the book, and this was the one Rolf was currently working on, dealt with the flayed human, this bloody abomination which, in truth, had never gone beyond the level of cannibalism.

It began with Swift's flippant remark about the unusual sight of the woman whose skin had been removed and reached its peak, as mentioned, in the discussion of the 'Modest Proposal'.

So far he had made good progress. If everything continued in this manner, the manuscript would be finished by the end of the holidays, ready to be shown to his publisher. He hoped that the contents would not come as too much of a shock.

That had been the state of play up to the Monday of the second week. Towards the evening things changed dramatically, though. The reason was a newly arrived couple with progeny who had moved into the room directly above Rolf and Regula. Rolf thought that they were hurling suitcases around; Regula believed it to be a pillow-fight. The noise rendered any thought of work impossible.

It was a Swiss German couple, and they had only one child — a boy of about four. As soon as he opened his mouth, he roared like a wild warrior in battle. If it got too much, his mother, a somewhat slovenly woman, shouted at him. The father shovelled his meals down, never said a word and clearly could not care less about what was going on around him.

Although the boy was still quite young, the family had come to dinner after Rolf and Regula, and they remained seated — a mere couple of tables away — past ten o'clock. Mind you, the little one hardly ever sat, but instead conducted races through the dining room, rolled on the floor, yelled, pestered other children, tripped up the waiters and turned the hotel's cutlery and porcelain into a drum kit.

They were very angry, Rolf even more than Regula. Their dinner was spoilt and on the way out Rolf asked the head waiter whether these people would be staying for a long time.

'Two weeks', he responded with a smile that asked for tolerance.

That did not bode well: they expected the worst for the rest of their holidays.

On the same evening, they had a second foretaste of just how bad it was likely to become. After the skirmish in the dining room there was no question of bedtime for the little ruffian. He came running into the hall, frisky as a puppy, and in the space of minutes had turned it into an obstacle course for himself and a number of other kids, who clearly shared his enthusiasm. The mother yelled every now and then, but without success, and the father read his paper, smoking a cigar unperturbed. Rolf burnt his throat with schnapps, because he gulped down the whole glass in one go, and Regula spilt her cup of verbena infusion over her blouse. They beat a hasty retreat to the lift.

Later on, there was half an hour's trampling, as if a herd of elephants was squabbling near a watering hole, and then it was silent. It stayed quiet throughout the night until about eight in the morning.

'At least that was a bonus', Regula and Rolf mused and felt that, if they asked the head waiter to allocate them a table, which was further away, they would surely cope.

That would, indeed, have been the case, if the ski school had lasted longer. However, it finished at four o'clock. At half past four, when Rolf was in the middle of writing, the mayhem above him resumed and continued without interruption until dinner time.

Rolf was desperate. He talked of leaving, privately cursed the hotel manager in vile terms and had not a single good word for the place anymore. Regula tried to calm him down, but could see herself that her arguments were weak. On the way to their meal, Rolf positioned himself in front of the concierge like a valiant hero ready for battle and demanded a different room. It was meant to be an ultimatum. The response, though regretful, was that they were overbooked. Had Regula not pulled his sleeve, Rolf would have turned abusive. His book was in danger.

Then, however, shortly before they entered the dining room, where the parents with their little terror had already settled down still only two tables away, his mood changed completely, in the wink of an eye. Instead of annoyance, a relaxed smile, with the thunderous lightning in his eyes replaced by almost sympathetic understanding; he showed delight in the food and pleasure in the wine instead of disgust and his usual pained expression. Regula noted this with amazement and allowed herself to be infected by the happier mood. If Rolf was well, she could not be otherwise.

'What on earth got into you?' she asked as they were leaving.

He took her by the hand, pulled her to the entrance hall and stood her in front of the notice board showing forthcoming events. He pointed to a pretty poster.

'Our small guests will be well looked after throughout the day by our experienced nursery nurse Jane Swift, who is fluent in English and German, as well as Swiss German.'
'I don't understand', said Regula.

'She is Irish. From Dublin. According to the hotel manager, she lives up here with a mountain farmer.'

'Why is this important?'

'Swift, my dear. I am working on a book on Swift.'

'And the mere fact that a Mrs Swift works in the house improves your mood dramatically and makes you beam in this way? I don't see the connection.'

'Never mind. Perhaps you'll understand when the book is out', Rolf said. 'And now go on and sit in our usual spot — I must go to the toilet; I'll be back in a moment.'

And, indeed, he was whistling as he walked off, something he had not done in years.

The next afternoon there was silence above their heads, enabling Rolf to work wonderfully well, and in the evening parents and the perpetual motion machine were missing.

'Have they gone?' Regula asked the waiter.

'Happen something with child', the Portuguese answered.

'Which has its advantages occasionally', Rolf remarked rubbing his hands in an unusually cheerful tone.

A man they had never seen approached them in the lobby.

'May I join you for a moment, please? Gadient, Cantonal Police. You are aware that a child has disappeared from the hotel? It is this one.' He pulled a picture from his pocket.

'You have not seen him anywhere today, late this afternoon?'

It was the little poltergeist.

'No', Regula said, and Rolf shook his head. 'We were in our room this afternoon. My husband was writing.'

'And nothing special struck you in connection with the child during the last few days?'

'Nothing. Except that he was — how shall I put it — a very lively kid', Rolf responded.

'You had a chat about that with the nursery nurse yesterday, didn't you?' the policeman said.

'Did you?' Regula was surprised.

'I ran into her when I went to the toilet and of course asked her whether she was related to the author of *Gulliver*, since I am writing a book about him at the moment. And then I added that I admired her nerves, faced with these wild brats.'

'Good nerves she definitely needs', the policeman said. 'This boy was in the ski school all day long. At four he was brought back and should have waited in the crèche for his parents' return from skiing on the Corvatsch. He never arrived, however.'

'Run away?' Rolf asked.

'Or perhaps kidnapped?' Regula asked.

'We are wary about speculating', the policeman retorted.

'Oh my word — whatever next!' Regula said later on. 'A child simply disappearing.'

'And yet even this has its advantages', Rolf smiled.

Regula looked at him. 'You have been in a weird mood since last night.'

The child remained unfound. Neither searches nor missing person announcements on the radio had any results. Rolf's work proceeded brilliantly: he wrote the last sentence on Friday evening; they would return home on Sunday. On Saturday they did their 'Walk Number Two' again: Crasta, Platta and through the ravine back to the village. Above the gorge they passed the farmhouse with the dry-cured meat hanging outside.

'Nearly forgot — I really wanted to get some!' Regula exclaimed and went in the direction of the house.

'Are you sure?' Rolf asked.

'Of course. You'll find such quality only in the mountains.'

Regula knocked at the door. A young woman opened. When Rolf saw her, he uttered a noise as if he was choking.

The young woman smiled. 'Is this a social visit?' she enquired.

'This is Jane Swift, the nursery nurse. I did not know that she lived here', Rolf said coughing.

'What a coincidence!' Regula said. 'We saw the Bündnerfleisch hanging outside and wanted to ask you to sell us a couple of pounds. We adore Bündnerfleisch.'

Jane Swift looked at Rolf, as if to ask whether he was serious. Then she said: 'Unfortunately, mine is not ready yet, and I have nothing else at the moment.'

'Well, too bad in that case', Rolf said, as if in a hurry.

'Is there another place around here where we could buy Bündnerfleisch, which has been dry-cured in the fresh air like yours?' Regula asked.

'Yes, our neighbour's is exactly the same. If you want to ask him. . .'

Regula was keen, but Rolf protested; he was too tired to traipse around in the snow for much longer. And when Regula insisted, he ranted a bit about how he was getting fed up with this Bündnerfleisch obsession. Regula shook her head and gave in. They made their way through the gorge back down to the village.

'It must be so hard for them to make a living', Regula said during dinner.

'Who?'

'The farmers up here. She has to look after children in the hotel for her family to survive. Did you see the kitchen? Really poor. And then they have two kids of their own, and the third appears to be on the way.'

'And the debts! The manager thinks that the husband has debts like a dog has fleas', Rolf said.

'Heavens, in addition to everything else! What a life! Nearly as dreadful as during your Jonathan Swift's times in Ireland', Regula said.

Our most holy couple

The second course of the Xmas Eve dinner had just been served. A lovely light lobster bisque decorated with angel wings.

'I trust they're not real', joked Madame with the off-the-shoulder dress at the third table on the left.

'But yes, of course! They shot three archangels and boiled them', her spouse responded from behind his slightly too high stiff collar.

'You nasty piece of work!' Madame called out, pretending to be horrified.

The string quartet played Boccherini.

'When I think how many malnourished Africans could be kept alive with half of what we are scoffing tonight', grumbled — mouth full — the fifteen-year old with his dirty trainers at the table of the banker.

'Can you not be quiet for once, at least tonight?' his father was about to say. He was, however, interrupted by the piercing scream emanating from the elderly lady in her little black sequined dress from near the window at the back of the room: 'My goodness me! Look at that!' pointing outside.

The eyes of all those who sat near the windows followed her index finger. In the second row, the son of the banker got up, driven by curiosity.

'Sit down, please!' his father hissed.

But others, mostly in the third row, followed his example. Even the waiters looked into the winter snowscape outside, instead of focusing on the plates, on the goblets for white and red wine, and on the water glasses.

'The picture! Just like an old Dutch Master', shouted the sequined lady who was said to be a patron of the arts.

'The Holy Family', mumbled the gentleman at the next table, an expert in pedagogy at a German university, clearly moved.

'Not quite yet, esteemed colleague', said the gynaecologist at the table in the second row, his tone firm and business-like.

By now, the hotel manager — making his way from one table to the next, as he did every night, but today in black tie, as befitted the occasion — turned to the window and saw the young couple slowly advance up the driveway in the light of streetlamps. He supported her; she could hardly move any more. Young people, almost children themselves and in any case definitely under twenty, and she with a belly that looked as if she had swallowed a globe.

'The girl is pregnant', the gynaecologist said somewhat superfluously.

'And barely able to continue!' the shrill voice of Madame, strapless, could be heard from the left.

The couple approached the main entrance. The director rushed out of the dining room, barely maintaining his decorum.

'Surely he won't want to send them away, not today!' the sequined lady said horrified and got up, ready to fight.

At the same time, Madame in the off-the-shoulder dress, and a few other guests, joined in.

'Should you not?' the wife of the gynaecologist asked quietly.

'I'd rather not impose', her husband replied.

'She seems to be scarcely fifteen', his wife impressed on him.

The fifteen-year old with the dirty trainers who sat at the banker's table giggled, while buttering himself a roll.

When the lady in the sequined little black dress and Madame in the off-the-shoulder outfit reached the entrance hall, followed by their spouses dressed up in uniform-like black tie, they saw the couple lean on the counter of the concierge and heard Arcangelo say, with the authority of the man who had all the keys in the hotel: 'I am sorry, but we're full.'

'This cannot be true!' Madame exclaimed.

'Certainly not!' her husband called out.

'Not on this night!' the sequined lady shouted.

'Ladies and gentlemen, please!' said the director.

'We do not have a single vacant room', the concierge said loudly and firmly.

'Arcangelo!' Madame admonished him accusingly.

'Don't be a monster', the lady in the little black dress added, while the husbands nodded vigorously.

'Not a single bed vacant anymore, not even in the staff quarters', insisted Arcangelo, having a heart made of stone.

'I cannot go on', breathed the girl and threatened to sink to the ground.

'Didn't I tell you to do something?' the gynaecologist's wife hissed in the direction of her husband.

Like most of the other guests they, too, had come into the foyer in order to see what was going on.

'But I haven't even got my things here', replied the gynaecologist.

'Nothing to be done', lamented the director wringing his hands hypocritically.

'In that case, I'll do something!' the elderly lady in the sequined little black dress called out. She approached the couple.

'Please come to the lift with me. Are you still strong enough? You can have my room, at least until the ambulance arrives.'

'There won't be time for a transport to hospital', the young man said, 'it will arrive any moment.'

The sequined lady strode ahead, the couple followed to the lift, past the Xmas tree in the entrance hall. Arcangelo had emerged from behind the counter.

'You will not prevent me, not you!' the lady threatened imperiously.

At that, Arcangelo stopped still, along with all the others, and stared with dopey eyes at the lift door closing and heard the elevator starting to move.

Now, noisy chatter erupted.

'You should have done something!' the gynaecologist's wife said.

'But what?' countered her husband.

'They get younger all the time', stated the wife of the professor of pedagogy.

Then the lift returned. The door opened and the spangled lady stepped out beaming like a heroine.

'Right, they're ok for the moment. Have you called a doctor and the ambulance? No? Heavens, what are you all waiting for then? Hurry up, Arcangelo, get on with it!'

Arcangelo ran behind the counter and made his way to the telephone, and the first guests returned to their tables in the dining room.

'We'd like to continue serving you, if that's convenient, ladies and gentlemen', the manager, arms aloft and clearly relieved, announced.

'They all think of nothing but food', the fifteen-year old with the dirty trainers muttered to himself. The quintet played 'Silent Night'.

The third course was loup de mer on a bed of leek. Most guests had already eaten it, with a degree of relief, when a group of men turned up: the village doctor, two ambulance crew and, without having been called, two police officers.

'This couple, where are they?' one of the policemen asked so loudly that he could be heard in the dining room.

'They have already used this trick in St Moritz', the other said.

The gynaecologist felt obliged to intervene: 'Remember that the girl is heavily pregnant', he called as he left.

'You obviously believe in the stork', the first policeman said to him. 'Pillows under the pullover, nothing more. As soon as they are allowed to go into a room, the pregnancy is miraculously over.'

'You mean. . . ?' the director stuttered.

'Let's go up', the policeman said firmly.

When they came down again, he grinned.

'What have I said? They must have parked their car nearby. Miles away by now. And three rooms ransacked.'

'My pearls!' screeched the lady with the sequins.

'Ours, too?' asked the gynaecologist's wife. 'It's right next door. . .'

After the police had left, having made a list of stolen goods and damage caused, and everyone was eating their dessert, the gynaecologist turned to his wife and said in a slightly grim tone: 'When I think of your diamond ring, I almost feel like one of the "Three Wise Men".'

The elderly lady in the little black dress said to Madame in her off-the-shoulder at the next table: 'It was a very impressive picture. Christmas has never touched me so much. It's just a pity about my pearls. . .'

And Madame, who was missing a platinum bracelet, added: 'It probably has to hurt a little bit for it to have such an impact, don't you think, my dear?'

Crack in the snow

'Where is my little black purse? Have you seen my little black purse?'

Walter had not seen Esther's little black purse anywhere.

'But you won't need a purse! I have got mine.'

'And if I take a different route?'

Esther's continuous search for freedom.

'Or if we lose each other? Without my own purse, I cannot even have a bowl of soup or a cup of coffee.'

At last she found it under the handkerchief on the bedside table. She counted the money. It was enough for soup and coffee.

Because of the search for the purse, they missed the cable car at nine twenty and could only get up to Furtschellas at nine forty. The sun was already burning on the mountainside and the snow had begun to turn slushy.

'The black run?' asked Walter.

The piste marked as black was the most difficult.

'I don't like that one', Esther said. 'In fact, I don't like any pistes. Come on, let's go through the forest.'

'And the avalanches?' Walter wanted to ask, but did not. She adored off-piste skiing.

Esther went through the clearing, as always ahead of him. Walter followed, as always at a distance.

Her skiing was truly heavenly. A feast for the eyes. Her slim body upright and the easy movement transferring itself effortlessly from the hips to the skis. Behind her, as if she were a comet, a tail of snow swirled in a wide arch. Far below, the ribbon of the frozen lakes was glittering like silver in the sunshine.

Walter did not ski any less well than Esther. He got through the clearing as safely as she had. Except that nobody would have turned around to watch him.

'Even from behind you can see her pleasure', people said, when she was skiing on a piste.

Esther was waiting at the point where the mountain pines gave out. She had come to a halt in a soft sweep. Walter drew his curve a bit more awkwardly, just above the last tree trunk.

In front of them, untouched and gleaming like diamonds, there was a vast field of snow, of which they knew that it ended above rocks a few hundred metres further down. They would have to stay slightly higher up to the left, towards the forest, in order to find the path between the pines, down to the bottom of the valley. First of all, however, the snowfield beckoned.

'I'd love to go straight down', Esther shouted, flushed with joy and excitement. 'All the way!' She pulled her pink hat with the band made of woolly flowers over her forehead.

At that moment, Walter spotted the crack. It opened up across the hillside, immediately below the last trees. Walter was on this side, Esther beyond.

The crack got bigger in seconds and turned into a crevice, and the slope was already beginning to slide at precisely the place where Esther stood.

'What's this? Hold on to me!' Esther screamed. She stretched out her hand to him.

Walter had no more than five seconds to stretch out his arm, grab Esther's hand and hang on to her with all his strength. The five seconds were an eternity, while Walter and his alter ego quarrelled with each other furiously. And as they squabbled, Walter saw an image on the screen of the sliding snowfield. He saw himself strolling hand in hand with a strange woman over the frozen lakes, looking up to the glittering white fields with her and wasting no thought on climbing up there to sketch their traces in the snow, but instead he saw how they returned to the hotel, sat in their warm and cosy room, took their books and read for a couple of hours before dinner.

The row was over, the decision taken. The pleading voice beyond the crack had lost. Walter did not extend his arm. It would have been too late, in any case. Esther was already too far away from him. She had turned her face to him and stared at him with wide-open eyes. Then she was swallowed up by the sliding torrent of snow.

'Walter!' the drawn-out scream could be heard through the thunder of the snow tumbling to the valley.

By the evening Esther had still not been found. When darkness fell, the search had to be abandoned. The experts told Walter that they had given up any hope.

He was very busy. Next of kin had to be informed, the family of Esther's brother, as well as that of his sister, and all their close friends, of course. The head of the rescue team wanted information. The management and staff of the hotel were touchingly concerned about him.

Around eleven o'clock that evening, he could at last withdraw to his room. He locked the door behind him. Esther's things were all over the place. He moved her clothes from the armchair onto her bed. Then he took the bottle of Scotch out of the fridge, poured himself a glass, sat in the chair, put his feet onto the little table, took a big swig, grabbed the book and opened it at the place where he had stopped reading the night before.

Death in Sils Maria

Schlegel had braced himself for the worst. What he saw now, though, exceeded everything by far. Where for heaven's sake had his daughter left her common sense? And, he added, with nearly more regret, her taste?

She had written to him in mid-January that she would not come to the Engadin alone this year. In her New Year's letter, in which she thanked him for the pearl earrings he had given her for Christmas, she wrote about a surprise that she had in store for him. He had suspected at once that it had something to do with men and that, this time, it was serious, given that Lilian talked about it already. Up to now she had always observed strict silence about such matters. Every now and then he had come across traces of men in her life. Last year, for example, when he had business in London and slept on the couch in Lilian's living room, he had cut himself shaving and, as he was looking for a plaster in the bathroom cupboard, came across not only a shaving kit but also a pair of cufflinks — beautiful ones, at that. The man appeared to have taste.

He would have been worried if Lilian had had no friends. She was, after all, twenty-seven, and he did not assume that her job with Brown & Masters, the international literary agency, which specialised in strategic studies, would fulfil her life's ambitions forever. He preferred not to know too much about the private aspect of her life and was looking forward to the ten days' annual skiing holidays they spent together in the Engadin.

People observing the older gentleman and the young woman, as they sat together at a table, laughing and talking, with him occasionally stroking her hand lovingly or kissing her, could have thought they were a couple. Boss and secretary, perhaps, who were on a few days' romantic holiday. And yet, they were father and daughter; he with a financial law firm at a very good Zurich address, and she, as already mentioned, in London, ever since she was seventeen.

They had got to know each other more closely only of late. Shortly after Lilian's birth, Schlegel's marriage had ended. He had relinquished all claims on the child. His wife had moved to Geneva with their daughter and married a South American millionaire, from whom she was now divorced again. The daughter had been sent to an expensive boarding school in the Engadin, where she stayed until shortly before graduating. At that stage her mother felt that she should improve her English and brought her to London.

Lilian had not met her father once in all those years, only his money, which arrived punctually. Then, a letter arrived in the post one day in December with the question whether she would like to join him in Sils Maria for a few days' winter sport in February. Naturally, he would pay for all costs, including the flight.

The holidays were a spectacular success. Since then, Lilian had considered her father a friend — they saw each other every year in the winter by the frozen lakes of the Engadin and she allowed herself to be spoilt by him for ten days.

Schlegel admitted to himself that there was a hint of jealousy in his judgement of his son-in-law. He was therefore determined not to make a fool of himself because of his feelings. Nevertheless, he did not want to believe that the devastating impression his daughter's friend made on him was only due to hurt manhood.

He knew from Lilian's letter that the man and he were nearly the same age. Schlegel was sixty-three, and the chap who would become his son-in-law, was sixty-four. In his view, this came close to incest. But he wanted to take a look at the old lecher, as he thought of him secretly, before he came to a verdict.

Everything else Lilian wrote should actually have been welcome to him as a father. The man was not a nobody. Sir Geoffrey Bell was sole owner of the prestigious publishing house Highway, Fitzwater and Bell, and connected with important firms, notably banks, as Schlegel easily discovered. He owned Cottingham Castle in Kent, a respectable estate with a stately home from the times of Elizabeth I. Bell's fortune was estimated in the hundreds of millions pound sterling. Sir Geoffrey had been divorced for three years. His marriage, to a well-known international polo player, had been childless.

All of this did not sound bad. Only the fact that he was sixty-four, a year older than himself, Schlegel found perverse — he was, after all, Lilian's father.

On the journey to the Engadin he had fought the disgusting pictures that were trying to appear in his mind vigorously and bravely. His daughter in bed with a geriatric. Trembling hands stroking her young flesh, Lilian, pushing a demented idiot in a wheelchair.

He forcefully suppressed the images. In the hotel, where he had been known for decades, he walked past his daughter's double room with contempt, trying not to think that she would share a bed with the old man from the next evening. When he had phoned her in London to ask, she had expressly insisted on a double room.

44

What confronted him at the St Moritz railway station at noon was, however, worse than anything that had appeared to him in his worst nightmares. Lilian got out of the train first. She had become even more beautiful with her light brown hair and a body that could take any man's breath away. Happiness makes people beautiful, Schlegel thought. But then a small fat man followed, at least a head and a half shorter than Lilian, with a pot belly on short legs and flat feet pointing outward like a duck's. His round head, balding and gleaming with sweat from the midday sun, was perched without a neck, directly on his shoulders. A nose like a potato, the mouth thick-lipped, perfectly formed for sucking oysters. Schlegel noticed soon that the man also talked as if he were devouring oysters in a competition. Sir Geoffrey was tucked in a fur coat, which made him look like an overweight infant.

What on earth had possessed Lilian? Schlegel asked himself and approached the two of them, only to realise at once that everything had changed.

In the past, Lilian had kissed him on the lips to greet him. Now there was nothing more than two fleeting air-pecks on the cheek. The man's hand felt like a boneless fish. Schlegel looked down on the sausage fingers and noticed the manicured nails, which stood out like sequins that had been attached to the end of the fingers. During the next few days he avoided touching these hands. He felt as if he might catch a nasty, contagious disease from them.

He had ordered a taxi, which was waiting for them outside the station. Lilian hurried ahead, Sir Geoffrey followed, waddling beside Schlegel. He bumped into him and his disgusting hands — he could not help himself thinking they

45

were pest-ridden — moved as if he was stroking her bottom. Then, he raised the fingers of his right hand to his swollen lips and smacked in such a disgusting way that Schlegel felt nauseous.

Fingertips on the lips combined with the smacking noise repeated themselves in the evening until Schlegel wanted to throw up. Once the gesture referred to the room, specifically the beds, then the wine, the main course of dinner and, particularly obnoxious, the young Italian waiter.

After the meal, all three had a whisky in the foyer. But Schlegel wanted to get this part of the evening over with as quickly as possible and said that he assumed they were tired from the long trip. He was looking forward to the room and the bed, responded Sir Geoffrey, slurping and smacking yet again, and raising the sausage ends of his right hand to his mouth.

Up to that time, saying goodnight outside Lilian's room used to be one of the most treasured moments of Schlegel's holidays. He was kissed on the lips, felt Lilian's proximity and could smell her scent.

Today there was nothing beyond a fleeting touch of the cheeks on the left and the right and a 'goodnight', in addition to the slimy anticipation of the fat clown. Schlegel hurried to his single room in despair, while imagining what the dwarf was now doing to his daughter.

That night, while he was lying in bed on the edge of going mad and quarrelling with a part of himself that could not stop horrific pictures as if produced by a pornographic printing firm, he decided to kill Sir Geoffrey. This was the only way to save Lilian from the worst disaster of her life. He did not know yet how he wanted to do it, but it had to happen during these days, before the catastrophe could not be averted.

In the bright light of the morning, he asked himself whether he had considered the consequences of his decision properly. He planned to observe the pair first and to come to a conclusion afterwards. He had to know whether Lilian was really serious about the fatso. It was, after all, possible that this was but a transient aberration.

But there was no sign of that; on the contrary. Lilian and her English gnome went, whenever possible, hand in hand, and Schlegel felt like a dog who had to watch when his adored mistress allowed herself to be smooched by a brute. The two exchanged loving glances even during meals and kissed every now and then. Schlegel lost his appetite.

When he was alone with his daughter for a moment on the third day – his future son-in-law suddenly had to go to the toilet and Schlegel immediately suspected that he was suffering from prostate problems – he tried to suss her out.

Lilian, however, laughed, put her hand on his arm and said: 'Jealous? Surely not, Dad.'

After that she flirted and canoodled even more shamelessly with this British Porky Pig.

Schlegel was sure that he would hurt his daughter, but he believed that a short sharp pain would be easier to bear than an endless life in despair. These thoughts reinforced his determination. He only had to wait for an opportune moment.

Days dragged on painfully: the gleaming white mountain chains turned themselves in front of his eyes into his daughter's stretched out body, and the clouds in the sky were Sir Geoffrey's lecherous fingers that stroked it.

However, as if heat were suddenly switching to cold, everything was soon only a question of technique. He invited Sir Geoffrey to join him on walks, when he was not accompanying his fiancée to the ski lift. He tried thus to gain his trust. That was not difficult. Sir Geoffrey behaved as if they were two conspirators and treated Schlegel, though a year younger, with the reverence that he thought one owed a father-in-law, but in a somewhat pitying manner.

After a week, an opportunity came up at last. The high pressure with the brilliant blue skies came to an end. Snow was forecast. Schlegel had only just prompted Sir Geoffrey to hire cross-country skis and to venture onto some easy loipen — Lilian preferred downhill skiing. At first, the Englishman acted very clumsily, but Schlegel did not give up. In the end, Sir Geoffrey even appeared to enjoy skiing, despite that the fact that it was only to impress his bride with his sporting accomplishments. During dinner he talked, fingertips at his lips, with slurping enthusiasm about his adventures and wished, at all costs, to return to the loipen next day.

They started at half past eleven after a plentiful breakfast. No sign of the sun and the clouds were low in the sky. But when Sir Geoffrey pulled a face, Schlegel made it a matter of honour. It took them an eternity to reach the Fextal. Fatso steamed like an overheating locomotive, but acted brave and Schlegel goaded him relentlessly by asking him every ten minutes whether they should not turn around. Sir Geoffrey would have been prepared to climb Mount Everest with his cross-country skis. In the restaurant at the end of the valley they were nearly the only guests. The Englishman was at the end of his strength and Schlegel was already asking himself whether it was even necessary to take special measures to get rid of him.

But nothing in the world would keep Sir Geoffrey down. Eagerly he spooned his bowl of barley soup, had Valtellina with it and, to finish the meal, a double Grappa with his coffee — foisted on him by Schlegel, who was aware that he would drink it if he warned him against it. The ruse worked.

On the way back, the snow fell in thick flakes as if sheets were coming down from the sky. Glad to see five, six metres of loipe in front of them, they glided onwards, Sir Geoffrey ahead, Schlegel urging him on, behind.

Wine and Grappa showed their effect. When they were only halfway, near the Hotel Sonne, Sir Geoffrey was already a wreck and wanted to take a rest, but Schlegel did not give in. It was fortunate that there was no horse-drawn carriage outside: Sir Geoffrey would not have moved another step.

Below the hotel, Schlegel steered him from the broad path to the right. Ten minutes later they found themselves in the spot where a footpath goes off the loipe and leads through a ravine to Sils. Visibility was zero, apart from the dense snow fall, which enclosed each of them as if they were in a cabin of frosted glass.

'This is a short-cut, not that easy, but we cannot miss the path', Schlegel shouted, fully aware that nobody would get down there on cross-country skis.

'Let's take it', Sir Geoffrey panted, audibly relieved.

'Go ahead, in that case! Off you go! I am sure nothing will happen.'

And fatso set off. He soon developed a speed at which he lost all control over his skis. Ahead of him, invisible in the snowfall, there was the abyss. He seemed to enjoy the wild, headlong schuss. Schlegel just saw how he raised his arms recklessly and heard him emit a noise that combined grunting with shouting for joy.

Then came the precipice over the rocks. Schlegel saw nothing else, heard nothing. No crashing, nothing. Everything covered in snow.

He took his time. He did not check, but turned around on the loipe and was back in Sils half an hour later. He enquired where the police station was. A further hour passed before a patrol left in the blizzard to scour the ravine. Sir Geoffrey was found, a sack full of broken bones and horribly disfigured.

Lilian froze when she returned from Furtschellas and Schlegel informed her, as gently as possible, of the accident. She withdrew to her room at once. Later on, she had to answer some questions from the police. She did so with a degree of composure, which shocked Schlegel. After they had had a small meal together, he accompanied her to her room. For the first time during the holidays, she kissed him on the lips.

Lilian did not want to see the body. She wished that he should be cremated and that the urn be transported to London. She asked her father to deal with the formalities on her behalf. She herself departed at once. Schlegel, closely involved both as father and as lawyer of course, accompanied her to the station in St Moritz. When the train departed they waved to each other cautiously. He returned to the hotel.

Schlegel needed two days to make all the arrangements. Every day he called London three times to be sure that Lilian did not do something stupid. On the third day he booked an evening flight from Zurich to London. He did not want to leave his daughter alone at this time. Then he travelled in the front on the passenger seat of the black hearse to Chur, where Sir Geoffrey's remains were cremated. He was asked whether he wanted to take the urn away with him. He said he would not, gave them the London address and paid the transport costs in advance. Then he drove on to Zurich. In his office there were only the usual letters. He had asked the taxi to wait for him and was therefore at home quickly. Mrs Ingold, his housekeeper, expressed her condolences and asked if he wanted to eat something. He shook his head.

'Please get my suitcase. I have to go to her.'

Mrs Ingold had put his post neatly on his desk. To the left the newspapers, in the middle printed matters, on the right personal letters. Nothing important in any of the piles of paper. With the faxes there was a letter. In English. He recognised Lilian's handwriting immediately. His hands trembled when he grabbed it. He read it.

My darling Papa,

I write to inform you that I spoke to Geoffrey's solicitor today. He confirmed what I knew already that Sir Geoffrey had made me his sole heir in case of his death. You do not, therefore, have to have any worries about your daughter anymore.

*I am very grateful that you have solved a problem for me; I was
sure you would do it.*

*I have come to know Mrs Ingold well enough to be sure that she
will not have anything to do with the fax machine; apart from that
she does not know English. Even so: please burn the letter in the
chimney when you have read it. Are you coming to the funeral? It
will take place on Wednesday week in St Paul's.*

With love and a kiss, your daughter Lilian

Schlegel looked up. Mrs Ingold had made a fire in the
chimney. He took the piece of paper, threw it in and waited
until it had been reduced to ashes. Then he called the
housekeeper.

'I shall, after all, only fly next week. What did you say was
for dinner?'

Goggles with black glasses

A swathe had been cut through the pine forest for the new loipe. TV and newspapers had published pictures of it in the summer: huge caterpillar vehicles, with roots and tree stumps torn out and splintered by the teeth of the digger, and the forest floor totally trampled.

Hilde, too, had seen the photos, and she had asked herself whether she could explain, if necessary, why she spent her skiing holidays precisely there, of all places. Having quickly balanced the pros and cons, common sense prevailed. She confirmed the booking. She knew well enough that these things happened in every ski resort. Trees were cut down everywhere. She did not wish to become disloyal to her holiday resort because of that: she had, after all, enjoyed the long cross-country skiing trails for years, with the glorious weather and a pleasant, not too expensive, hotel. 'Now more than ever', she said to herself with a touch of defiance. Eventually, she was looking forward to the skiing holidays again: they meant more to her than Italian beaches or Finnish lakes in the summer.

Now Hilde stood on her cross-country skis where the pine forest started, behind her the newly cut swathe, which gave the impression of having always been there; she looked ahead onto the white expanse of the frozen lake. She soaked up the vastness of the high mountain valley and let the sun burn her forehead.

The new loipe was indeed an asset. Hilde even thought that it would have been a pity not to go ahead. What were a few trees compared to this view, after all. It was unique!

Hilde stopped herself dreaming and went on, down the slope and into the flat plain of the snow-covered, icy lake. Next to the two tracks for the skiers there was a footpath for walkers. Although it was high season, the holidaymakers were rather thinly spread. One could have believed oneself alone in the world. Hilde loved this feeling. She loathed nothing more than crowds.

Two hundred metres in front of her, a lonely figure wandered ahead, going in the same direction as she was. She could not tell, against the light, whether it was a man or a woman. There were another fifty metres between this shadow, striding along eagerly, and the next one. Far ahead, Hilde spotted two figures emerge on the path. They seemed to stand still. At that point, to the left of the loipe, there was a place that had been fenced off with a red plastic tape, which could be seen from a great distance. The lake was probably not properly frozen there.

Hilde had looked into the distance for too long and lost her balance over a bumpy patch. She very nearly fell over and clearly needed to concentrate on the loipe.

When she looked up again, the picture in front of her had changed. The first skier had already passed the two hikers. Hilde saw him move far ahead. But the second one, who had been closer? Where was the second skier? She could not detect him anywhere. She only noticed that one of the two pedestrians had crossed the loipe and approached the edge of the water hole where he performed a kind of dance. Hilde stopped still. Was he waving for help? The second skier had not, by any chance —?

But if the skier had fallen into the water hole, the hiker would surely not cross the loipe again and calmly join the other one.

What, then, had happened up ahead? Probably nothing, Hilde thought to herself, and because she heard someone come up behind her, she proceeded. She had probably been wrong. The skier she saw glide along far beyond the two hikers was not the first, but must be the second. She had not considered the speed of these young people. The first had no doubt gone much further and had by now become part of the dark bundle of skiers on the horizon. Two skiers overtook her from behind. Hilde attached herself to them and proceeded in their wake for quite some distance.

When they had reached the level of the water hole, the two hikers were still standing there. A man and a woman. Hilde was first struck by their odd clothes. Their garments were mostly hand-knitted and their ski boots ancient, with gleaming brass nails at the sides, familiar from photos of her parents. Both were wearing white woolly hats, stretched over their heads so tightly that they appeared to be bald. The most striking thing about them was their goggles. Old-fashioned spectacles with black glasses in white frames. They made their faces look chalk-white. Both turned their heads towards the three skiers, and the goggles, the hats and the lips, which had been painted white to protect them against the harm of the sun, made their faces appear like skulls.

Hilde shuddered and hurried on, so as not to lag behind the two other skiers, although they were too fast for her. She was soon out of breath, had to slow down and eventually stop altogether. She hardly dared look back. But she did not have to be frightened. The two hikers now stood by the water hole and between them and Hilde there were at least half a dozen people. The two stood there like aliens: two masked figures among all the unmasked.

By the evening, Hilde had forgotten the encounter. Acquaintances invited her to join them at their table. She was pleased to accept their offer and the three of them enthused about the new loipe.

They had reached dessert, when another guest, also a keen cross-country skier, approached them and asked whether they had already heard.

'No. What?'

'A cross-country skier has been missing since this afternoon. Probably sunk into ice where the lake is not completely frozen.'

Hilde was shocked.

The second skier! It must be him. Though the hotel guest said that nothing specific was known. Apparently there were no witnesses.

The two hikers! Hilde suddenly thought. If it was that place and if the missing person was the second cross-country skier, then the man and the woman with the old-fashioned goggles must have seen how he disappeared into the lake. But the two had not yet come forward as witnesses. So, the accident had not taken place at that water hole or, on the other hand… Shivering, Hilde thought of what had looked like a tribal dance when she had observed the gesticulation from afar — the two must surely be connected with the disappearance of the skier.

'You mustn't be frightened, Miss Hilde', her friend said, laughing. 'The ice is being checked very carefully and the critical patches are all clearly marked. If someone falls through and drowns, it can only be because they have not kept away from the barriers. Unfortunately, there are always careless people. People, who believe that bans apply to everyone but them. They then have to suffer the consequences.'

Hilde went to her room early. Should she notify the police of her observations? But what had she actually observed? She could not even say, she told herself, whether there had been a trail from the loipe to the water hole. Had the skier in front of her left the loipe, he would have left a trail in the soft snow. When she had reached the level of the water hole, she had only looked at the two hikers in their weird get-up. Home-dyed wool. Tree-huggers. Had there not been protests in the summer against the destruction of the trees for the sake of the new loipe? And the threats on the flyers? Hilde had read about it. She slept badly that night.

In the morning she read in the paper that the missing skier had not yet been found. The leader of the rescue team felt that the likelihood of him being discovered during the thawing period was small, if indeed he had disappeared in the lake.

The friends from last night invited her to join them. Again, they took the path through the new cutting, but on the lake they kept to the left-hand side where a fresh loipe had been made early in the morning. It was less sunny than on the previous day. In Maloja, they sat on the hotel terrace and had a trout cooked on the grill. Hilde found it all very agreeable.

While her friend went to the toilet and her husband paid the bill, Hilde was by herself at the table for a few minutes and gazed out into the dazzling snowy landscape, into the gathering clouds, onto the sides of the mountains and the road in front of the restaurant. At that moment, she spotted yesterday's two hikers pass. Dressed the same way, their pale faces under the white hats, which were tightly pulled over the head, the goggles with the round black glasses in their white frames. They glanced over to Hilde and disappeared at the same moment.

Hilde did not know whether she had really emitted a scream or whether she had only screamed inwardly. At that very moment, her friends returned.

'We must hurry. It will start snowing soon', the husband said. They broke up in a rush, not least because Hilde had booked a session in the sauna for half past four.

Before too long, the sun disappeared behind the clouds and snow began falling. There were only few people still around. They had done about three-quarters of the distance when her friend lost one of her skis. They stopped. Her husband investigated the damage and reckoned that he should try to put a makeshift ski binding together with a boot lace. His wife looked at her watch.

'It's already half past three. Hilde; you must run ahead, if you don't want to miss your sauna.'

Hilde was thus alone for the final stretch, two-hundred metres in front of her a solitary skier. Near the cordoned-off spot with the red barrier by the wayside there were, lo and behold, the two skulls, woolly hats tightly pulled over their heads, white painted lips, round goggles with the black glasses and white frames. When the skier in front of Hilde arrived there, it seemed as if a scuffle had broken out. She thought she heard a suppressed scream. Was that flash a knife?

The skier was pushed, came off the loipe towards the water hole and sank. Hilde heard nothing. When she forced herself to avert her eyes from the water hole, the two skulls were no longer visible.

She did not know how she got to the hotel, a trembling bundle of fear. Instead of going to the sauna, she skied directly to the police station and told them with much excitement and confusion what she had seen. The policeman was friendly and understanding, nearly too friendly, with the result that Hilde did not feel he was taking her seriously. She had to tell him everything twice, including the events of the previous day, and he made a few notes. Then he took the phone and talked in Romansh[3] for a long time.

'Did you see a trail of blood by the water hole?' he asked after he had put the phone down.

She could not tell.

They would see what had to be done, the policeman said. As far as he knew, yesterday's missing person had re-appeared.

With that, Hilde was dismissed. Her statement did not carry much weight, although she had actually been able to describe the perpetrators!

The snow had stopped falling and dusk had begun to descend when Hilde left the police station. The streets were nearly empty. Hotel guests were changing for dinner.

Hilde did not take the path to the hotel. She had to be certain. Was there a trail from the loipe to the water hole? Could one

---

[3] He must have talked in the local language assuming that Hilde, a tourist, would not understand him.

see blood? It would still be visible now. If snow fell during the night, the tracks would be erased by the morning.

Hilde put on her skis and left the well-lit road. Her eyes had to get used to the dark. She noticed then how the snow brightened up the night. She found the loipe without difficulty. It seemed to her as if she were moving more than ever in a state of weightlessness, fast like the youngsters, although she had an exhausting day behind her.

Soon she was near the water hole. And there, fifty metres ahead of her, to the right of the loipe, she saw one of the two skulls, with the woolly hat, the white lips, the black, white-framed goggles. Hilde stopped still. She did not dare to pass the figure. Then she heard behind her the scrunching steps in the snow, and when she turned around she recognised the second skull, who approached in a measured pace. She had to evade them and head to the left!

She started skiing again, now away from the loipe, which was more difficult. But the skull behind her was faster. Not even fifty metres further on, she saw how he approached her at an angle from the left and behind her. The second now advanced from the right. Hilde had to change direction once again. She took the only path left open. When she recognised the red barrier tape in front of her, she hoped that the water hole had closed itself in the cold temperatures of the evening. She could not escape them. She tore the ribbon. She felt the water soaking her boots. She felt a vast bottomlessness beneath her, and she sank down.

Surprising that the water was not much colder. She thought of the two white heads with the black goggle holes behind her and then remembered that she had not looked for the trail of the cross country skier, as she had intended. Then Hilde did not feel anything anymore.

In the cold, starry, clear night, the water hole in the lake froze up and remained frozen for the rest of the winter.

An old acquaintance

On Tuesday, Burger had an appointment with the PR agency and another one with the photographer who was going to make a poster of him that could be used for global advertising. On Wednesday morning, he finished off some stuff in his office and then reached some tactical agreements with the party president in a long telephone conversation. In the early afternoon, he and his wife drove to the Engadin for twelve days.

When they returned, the election campaign would start. Burger, a lawyer in a prestigious legal practice, and for two terms a member of the cantonal parliament, had been nominated by his party as a candidate for the vacant seat on the governing council. He fancied his chances. The opposition party had been forced to withdraw their first candidate after media reports of nepotism. The second candidate, nominated in an embarrassing hurry, cut a rather weak figure. Nevertheless, campaigning was not going to be a walk in the park.

They arrived in the hotel shortly after 5 o'clock and moved into the same room as every year. Unpack, lie down for a little nap, hot bath, get changed for dinner. They were both hungry and looking forward to the light and healthy cuisine, to the espresso in the hall after dinner, even to the jingling of the piano, although they never danced. Shortly before half past seven, they got to the dining room.

The head waiter came running, shook their hands, asked how they were — he was fine, thank you — and led them to the usual table in the corner, near the exit. They were not the last, but most guests were already seated and were eating. They pulled the menu from the elaborately folded napkins and read, on the left in French, on the right in German. The fact that 'consommé' turned into 'Kraftbrühe' ('beef tea') amused Burger's wife again, just like every year. Four courses, always with three choices. Burger's wife chose the soup, fish, and lamb chops, while Burger decided on carrot juice instead of soup, also followed by fish and then roast veal. In the meantime, the head waiter had discreetly pushed the wine list towards Burger. Burger opened it, and the names, all rich in tradition, appeared to him like a road map to paradise. White with the fish, red with the meat. Burger ordered a bottle of Sancerre and a bottle of Valtellina Riserva Speciale. The head waiter nodded his approval of both.

Now they were waiting for the first course. They leant back in their chairs, simultaneously unfolding their napkins, and let their eyes roam over the dining room, recognising the odd face from the past, and reassuring each other how much they enjoyed being back.

The head waiter brought the two bottles of wine and some mineral water. He poured a glass of white for Burger to taste. Burger took the glass, swirled it slightly and raised it to his lips to test. The wine was ok.

'You'll like it. It has a pleasant, subtle acidity, which is very refreshing', he said to his wife, still holding his glass.

The head waiter turned to Burger's wife and poured her a glass. Burger himself had another sip of the tasting glass, and then the waiter filled it up, too.

He was about to put the glass down and look over the rim into the dining room when he recognised Lola. That is, he only saw the wild shock of carefully teased black hair, but it was Lola. Without a doubt.

Burger put the glass down and had to hold on to the stem. An unsuspected, evil perspective opened up. Burger heard the waiter's question as to whether he should open the Valtellina now as if in a haze. He only nodded when his wife looked at him slightly puzzled. It was extremely important that she didn't notice anything.

Burger dared cast another glance in the direction. Yes, that was unquestionably Lola, sitting — with her back to them — at the table of an older, discreetly dressed lady. The hair, the garish, brightly coloured dress, the broad hips; all of that belonged to Lola.

The young Portuguese waiter brought the soup for Burger's wife and the glass of carrot juice, the colour of red lead, for Burger himself, wishing them 'bon appétit'.

'Thank you', replied Burger and his wife politely, and in harmony — like a choir. They nodded 'bon appétit' to each other. Burger was glad that they were busy. He had to plan.

A meeting with Lola was out of the question. No, not because of his wife. She was sensible and not jealous. But because of the election.

Lola was attractive, beautiful and electrifyingly erotic, but she could be unbelievably loud and common. When she opened her mouth, vulgar obscenities crossed her lips. Burger had found that funny for a short time. Now he was horrified at the thought.

He had to keep an eye on Lola. As far as he could tell, she and her companion were being served the main course. How she tilted her head slightly towards the waiter! He imagined the pupils in the corners of her eyes. Her astonished cat-like eyes. He had to take particular care the moment she got up. When she left the room she would, inevitably, have to go past their table. At that point Burger had to rise as fast as possible, before she spotted him, and escape.

He imagined her approaching him. She would notice him, emit a screech of utter surprise, throw her arms up in the air and sprint towards him — her cheap bling startled into gruesome clattering noises — in order to fling her arms around his neck and sit on his knees.

'My little Bobby, are you here, too!?'

His wife's face. And all the faces turning round.

'The soup is flowing directly into my soul', Burger's wife said. 'How was your carrot juice?'

How had his carrot juice been? Had he already drunk it?

'Excellent', he said. 'Freshly squeezed.'

Before Burger grabbed his white wine glass again, he glanced over there once more — in disbelief. Her black hair poured over her shoulders like a wild torrent. A ridiculous pink bow gleamed on her neck as if she were a lap dog.

'Cheers! Happy holidays! Rest and relaxation! And, later on, good luck', Burger's wife toasted him.

'All the best to you, too', he responded.

They clinked glasses and let the ring of the crystal fade away into the chatter of the room.

In the meantime, the Portuguese cleared the soup bowl and the juice glass. Burger reckoned that Lola might spring into action at any moment, before he could do anything about it. With her upbringing, he would not put it past her that she would suddenly jump from the table to run outside, having remembered that she had to call a friend.

Burger peered in her direction. There sat a danger for his political career, a banana skin on his path to becoming a member of the national governing council. In these morally nit-picking times, when the media were greedy for reports of sexual affairs, he would be sunk if it came out that he knew her.

The waiter served the second course. Salmon on spinach. Burger raised his glass again. Unsuspecting, his wife toasted back.

In Burger's mind, the gutter press already had headlines on the front pages of the tabloids. 'Governing council candidate in brothel scandal: Lola tells all!' Once the journalists got her to talk, and that would not be difficult, she could do him in. 'He was a regular client in my salon. Yes, sado-masochism included. Lola, squeezed into tight leathers, legs straddled, swinging a whip. He shuddered.

'Are you cold?' his wife asked.

'Not too warm, anyway', he replied.

Through his connections in the property market, he had arranged for her to get a bigger apartment, as a farewell gift, so to speak. Subsequently, he had not shown himself anymore, but decided one morning that there must be an end.

'Pity that there are bones in the fish', his wife said, as she put one on the edge of the plate. 'But apart from that the cuisine is wonderful again.' He nearly choked on a bone and quickly gulped down some wine.

At the table over there, the remains of the main course were cleared away. But even if they took their time over dessert, they would be finished with dinner first. The head waiter came to pour the Valtellina for him to test. He did not taste anything. The waiter filled the glasses and toasted them with words 'Your health'!

The first time Burger had met Lola was in the chambers of a colleague at Bellevue in the expensive business centre of Zurich.

'Our new apprentice', his colleague noted when he saw how difficult it was for Burger to take his eyes off the girl's figure. 'By the way, she earns her pocket money with striptease.'

Even then she was a little prone to show her curves. He made a mental note of the venue, but did not go there the same evening. He let a whole month go by. When he then saw her on stage under the red lights, he was simultaneously gripped by her beauty and shocked by the vulgarity of her performance. He asked her to join him at his table and after that he drove with her to her apartment.

From that day onwards, he picked her up from the club, first once a week, soon every night. He ordered her to do everything in her repertoire: the stuff with the whips, the tight leathers, the handcuffs and the sharp needles drawing blood.

His wife got her lamb chops, he his roast veal. The waiter poured him another refill. You must not drink too much, you need a clear head, he said to himself.

It appeared that his wife had not been aware of his adventures at the time. She had started to devote herself to social issues and evidently found fulfilment there.

One night Lola had said to him: 'I want my own salon.'

'And your apprenticeship?'

'I chucked that. I earn more this way.'

The traces of other men didn't annoy him, who normally tended to be the jealous type. On the contrary. They had the effect of stimulants.

'Couldn't you do something for me? You do, after all, have connections.'

He did indeed. And made the necessary arrangements. And one morning, getting up, as his naked feet touched the coarse rug in the marital bedroom, he decided not to visit her anymore. No explanation on his part. No question on hers. They had not come across each other since then.

'Will you give me some more water, please?' his wife asked.

He poured her some.

In the meantime she had turned into a whore, well-known throughout town. Three or four years ago there had been an incident with a gang of pimps. They threw her furniture out of the window because she didn't want to work with them anymore. He had tried to read about it as if she were a total stranger. At the time, she had told a journalist that her clientele included people from the best circles and that she could well imagine someone wanted to drive her out of town. He took this as a threat aimed at him.

He drank and peered in her direction over the rim of his glass. She must have stewed in her feelings of fury and revenge for all those years. Who knows what she had been hoping for. She would, seeing him sitting here, not hesitate to make the most of the situation and send him to his doom — uncouth and vulgar as she was.

He had to talk to her. Invite her for a walk. To the bridge over the River Inn, and then push her in. That would be his salvation. The only possible solution.

He put the wine glass back on the table and turned his attention again to the roast veal. In doing so, he had lost sight of Lola for a moment too long. Because when he looked up, she was less than ten metres away. She came directly towards him. He had the feeling that the floor under him was wobbling. Getting up and running away was no longer an option. Too late. She approached, hips swaying, dress too skimpy and much too short, tarted up like a flag ship, hair teased to a tower, gravel pits full of bling covering her breasts. He was lost.

And then she was gone. Nothing had happened. No hysterical scream, no screeching call of recognition, no revengeful approach, nothing. She stalked past him as if he was one of the banal pieces of furniture in the dining room, without even casting a single glance at him.

He struggled not to let anything show. The red wine glass trembled slightly in his hand. They ordered dessert, and his wife reminded him of last year's holidays. They left the dining room a quarter of an hour after Lola.

Just like every evening, he left the room key at the front desk before they had their espresso in the foyer. His wife went ahead to occupy a table.

'This has been handed in for you.' The porter presented him with a small folded slip of paper.

Burger opened it and recognised Lola's handwriting. 'Don't worry. I'll leave tomorrow morning. L.'

He read the note twice. Then he tore it into small pieces and threw it into the wastepaper basket.

His wife had found a free table with two comfortable chairs. He sat next to her. When the waitress came, they both ordered an espresso.

'And a grappa?' the waitress asked, because he always drank a grappa after dinner.

'Yes, please — a double. And a Davidoff', he replied.

'What on earth is up?' his wife enquired.

'Feeling good. Just as one does on holiday', Burger retorted.

Avalanche barrier

There was every prospect for yet another glorious winter day. Andy got up early and took the cable car up to the top. He had his stuff in the rucksack: camera, tripod and all the other equipment he needed for work, and the skins as well. He did not want, like the rest of them, to speed down the prepared pistes as soon as he reached the top, but wanted to climb a bit first, perhaps half an hour, at least as far as the avalanche barrier. The view from there was even more beautiful, and one could believe oneself alone in the world.

At the summit station he greeted Johann, who had been working in the ticket office for years.

'I'll scramble up to the barrier', he told him.

'Enjoy!' Johann shouted behind the window.

The snow started to become slushy in the heat of the sun. Andy trudged uphill and felt like an ant on a white wall. He saw an animal trail, which drew a peculiar pattern into the snow, much like hieroglyphs. He very nearly stopped to get his camera out. But he figured that he might then lose the energy to continue climbing.

It took him almost half an hour to get to the barrier. Iron girders embedded in concrete foundations caught the masses of snow on the steep slopes above and prevented them from burying the piste, and possibly even the mountain station. This way, every year, one or two avalanches were held back. Each one of them, Andy knew, had a name, as if it were a live animal.

The snow had melted around the foundations. Andy took his skis off, leant the rucksack against an iron girder, detached the skins and rolled them up. There would be charming pictures, the vast white mountain scenery, broken by the pattern of the rafters. In order to take the photographs, he climbed onto one of the concrete blocks and squeezed himself, with camera and tripod, through the girders. It was not easy and he knew, of course, that it was dangerous. Should the snow slide above him, he would be crushed to death. But he was confident that nothing would happen.

This was a revelation. He allowed the iron fencing to chop the landscape into big and small, vertical and oblique, parallel and slanted pieces. It should look like a jigsaw, with puzzle pieces that belonged together but, at the same time, didn't actually fit. He worked like someone possessed. At one time he let the circle of peaks dissolve and keep the rafters in sharp focus; another time the pillars were blurred in the foreground and the mountains razor sharp. Never before had he seen this scenery 'licked clean', so to speak, of all the photography, never had it appeared so new, so rebellious, so beautiful to him. Only when he had used up all the film he had brought with him, did he stop. It turned into a triumphal downhill run, spoils in the rucksack.

He didn't want to wait for the end of his holidays. A local colleague allowed him to use his studio on his afternoon off. The series took his breath away.

While sorting through the pictures, his eyes suddenly caught a detail in one of them: the concrete foundation was very clearly visible in the foreground. There was a deep tear in the concrete, with the iron girder appearing only loosely inserted in the block by now.

Andy looked for the other pictures on which the foreground was in focus and checked out the foundations there, too. He found three more damaged concrete blocks.

To be certain, he enlarged the sections. They also showed the neglected state of the avalanche barrier.

He did not mention this to his colleague. But neither could he keep completely quiet about it. The big avalanches with the illustrious names had not yet come down, but when they pushed against the iron girders, the foundations would probably break. It was unimaginable what would happen if the avalanches, together with the metal fencing, thundered down the busy piste.

He had taken a few of photographs for the tourism director before and arranged an appointment with him now. He packed the enlargements, together with the whole series.

'Wonderful pictures', the director raved.

'Please look at the foundations. All torn. I wonder whether they could withstand the pressure when the avalanches come.'

'Oh well', retorted the director, 'could be worse. That's an old story. I can assure you, there is no danger.'

'Really? It seems to me —'

'Quite amazing pictures! Will you leave them with me until tomorrow?'

Andy tried once again to draw the director's attention to the damaged foundations. He, however, did not listen to him.

'These photographs. We've got to make use of them. For something major. By the way: don't even think of telling the media about this nonsense of the foundations. You would be laughed at', he said and ushered him out of the door.

The following afternoon, Andy, the director and the president of tourism had a meeting around the conference table in the office of the director. Laid out, in front of them, the photographs. Except for the enlargements.

'Would it not be appropriate to shut the piste?' Andy asked.

'Rubbish, in the middle of the season', the president grumbled. 'These things hold up; we vouch for that. We are the experts here.'

'Your photographs, however', the director began again, 'are a knockout! A truly new aspect of the village, of the whole valley, indeed. We suggest we use them to build our new marketing strategy for the winter season on them. What do you say? We'd offer you a pre-contract.'

Of course, this was a deal for him. The deal he had been waiting for. The deal that would bring in the big money. Finished with the freelance, hand-to-mouth existence, chasing after petty local news.

'At the same time, at the start of the season, we'll organise an exhibition of the whole series. Congratulations; this will be a success.'

He moved from his bed and breakfast accommodation into a four-star hotel the same day and stayed ten nights instead of six, avoiding only the cable car that led to the run with the avalanche barrier.

Until way into the summer season, he repeatedly went up into the mountains. There was a lot of work to do. He could not complain about lack of new commissions. The advertising campaign was successful; the director had not exaggerated. His work found a wide echo in the media.

The opening of the exhibition took place on a dazzlingly beautiful day at the end of January, a day as marvellous as the one of his climb to the avalanche barrier. Andy basked in the general approbation and drank a lot of white wine, until he felt enveloped by a light haze.

He saw the director approach with open arms and heard him call his name loudly. The director pointed to one of the pictures, where the iron girder with the concrete foundation could be seen more than clearly in the foreground, in front of the mountains, which were blurred, further back. He heard the director whisper into his ear: 'It held up, didn't it? What a smart alec you were, coming out with that nonsense!'

At this very moment, the picture began to fade in front of his eyes, as if a white roller was moving over it from top to bottom, and outside a thunder started to rumble, the like of which he had never heard in his life before.

Ibex through binoculars

'Really?' Mrs Bär said to old Vontobel, as she chatted with him and his daughter in the foyer of the hotel for a few minutes after breakfast. 'You have never seen ibex?'

Old Vontobel shook his head.

'You have come here — for how many years?'

'Twenty-one', Vontobel's daughter Erna replied.

'You have spent your holidays here for twenty-one years, have a room with mountain view and have never seen ibex!'

Mrs Bär could hardly believe it. Her husband nudged her in the sides to get her to quieten down a bit.

'But have you not got binoculars?' she asked, now nearly whispering.

'No', responded old Vontobel.

'In that case, I'll lend you mine', Mrs Bär announced, volume turned to maximum again. 'If you wait, I'll bring them down at once.'

And off she went, up the stairs. Less than three minutes later, she was back.

'You're very welcome to keep them for the next few days. You'll see that the sight of these majestic animals drives people mad with enthusiasm.'

And she explained in great detail and with much noise how he should use the binoculars.

Old Vontobel already regretted not having refused her offer at once. What on earth should he do with ibex? For twenty-one years, he had been coming here to have a three-week holiday, had never known anything about ibex and had never missed them either. Why should he now suddenly observe ibex? And why should he even become mad about these beasts, given that, in truth, he could not care less about them. Quite apart from this, he had an exceptionally exciting Eric Ambler novel on the go and found it very difficult to tear himself away from it at mealtimes. But Vontobel was a polite person, the product of a good, middle-class upbringing spanning several generations. He therefore accepted Mrs Bär's binoculars with thanks and said how happy he was to be able to see these unusually wonderful animals at last, and he promised to look out for them diligently.

The day was, however, extremely bad for observing ibex: thick snow had been falling since early morning. The mountains were draped in clouds and fog, which reached deep down into the valley. Erna put on her fashionable blue synthetic outfit. Caflisch, the skiing teacher who had given her lessons for years, had a day off and she therefore joined the Rosenthals, who were planning to walk all the way to Samedan and back.

This promised to be a proper, but not too strenuous tour for Erna, who was, after all, forty-six by now. Vontobel had given up skiing and had for a long time also left his ice skates at home. A good half hour through the snow each day, leaning on his stick and Erna's arm, was sufficient for him.

But now, after they had all gone, he was in an excellent mood. He put Mrs Bär's binoculars over his shoulder and took the cable car up the mountain. In his cosy and warm room, which smelled of pine wood, he would settle down near the window and continue reading his novel. Around two o'clock he would feel slightly thirsty and get the half bottle of bubbly from the fridge. That was as good as a day in the sun.

Today, in this weather, he would not leave the house at all, particularly as Erna would only return around four o'clock. He would have finished the novel by the evening, and Erna would be able to return it to the library before dinner and get a new one.

Once he reached the top, Vontobel was confronted by a serious problem. Which of the two windows of his room should he choose? The one that faced west would be brighter, even when, like today, the sun was not shining. The armchair with the upholstered backrest was there and, next to it, the little round table. And on that table was the novel, open at the place where Vontobel had stopped reading. The other window faced north, towards the rocks.

Ambler beckoned. Vontobel had reached a critical point and he, old lawyer and retired high court judge, much enjoyed following the action and seeing how the noose tightened.

On the other hand, he was an exceedingly decent fellow. As he had practically promised Mrs Bär to be on the lookout for ibex with her binoculars, he also wanted to do it. Thus, he thought, better get on with it straightaway, without delay. Then he could return to Ambler with a good conscience and all the happier for it.

Vontobel settled himself next to the north-facing window and held the binoculars to his eyes. At first he only saw a milky veil. He fiddled with the two lenses until he could distinguish the branches of the pines from individual boulders jutting out from the snow.

As diligently as he used to study his papers, he scanned the mountainside, particularly around the foot of the rocks, because he assumed the ibex would be sheltering there from the bad weather. But he could not make out any ibex, not a single one. Instead, he suddenly recognised a trail that led straight across the snow field. It was the track of a skier.

Vontobel was overjoyed. Obviously, they still existed, the lonely ski-wanderers who climbed up mountainsides, skins attached, just as he had done in his youth. He followed the track with his binoculars. There he was: a man who strode out. He carried a rucksack and — Vontobel adjusted the binoculars — indeed: the man had a gun! A hunting rifle, as Vontobel could just about see, before the man disappeared behind a group of pine trees. Was the shooting season not long over?

The lawyer in Vontobel began to stir. If the alpine hunting season was over and a man was clambering around the rocks where ibex lived, he had to be a poacher, and thus had to be reported, arrested and convicted.

Vontobel knew that a great deal of unauthorised hunting took place in the region and that the locals had differing views on the matter. Poachers were considered serious criminals — their tales often ending in blood and gore — but, at the same time, they were also admired as heroes by some, as defenders of a free and unrestricted hunt; that symbol of freedom.

Personally, Vontobel had never been a hunter, though he counted many hunters among his friends. They all had, if he thought about it, a streak of the adventurous, a thirst for freedom, a deep-seated unpredictability. And he knew from their stories that a hunt in the lowlands could not be compared to one in the high mountains, particularly in the Grisons.

Lo and behold: the first time he looks for ibex, a poacher comes into view. Nonsense, poacher, Vontobel thought. Surely, he'll be the game warden. He had put the binoculars onto the windowsill because his eyes had begun to water. Now he picked the binoculars up again and searched once more for the group of pine trees to check whether he could spot the hunter there. It was too late. The man must have left through the snow field. Vontobel saw the new trail. It passed through the woods further down.

Vontobel put the binoculars away and moved over to the other window to his book. As impatient as he had been to continue reading his novel, it had now lost its attraction. Time and again the skier moved straight through the sentences with his hunting rifle. He could not be chased away. Finally, Vontobel shut Ambler angrily with a snap. He went to the phone and called the municipal administration. A nice lady confirmed that the hunting season was over. The man in charge? His name was Giovanelli. She gave Vontobel the number.

Should he really call? Would that not give the impression that an old man wanted to throw his weight around. There was nothing Vontobel feared as much as looking as if he suffered from dementia. If this, however, was indeed a case of poaching, then it was his civic duty to report what he had observed, so that the criminal's activities could be stopped.

Whether it was a poacher or an official in control of the hunting season could only be established by Vontobel making a phone call. If Giovanelli was at home, then Vontobel must have spotted a poacher. If Giovanelli was not at home, everything was possible. It could be him who was following the ibex or it could be an unauthorised individual.

Vontobel dialled the number and let it ring at least ten times. No response from Giovanelli.

At half past four, Erna returned. She poked her head round his door, face flushed from the wind, and then proceeded to have a bath. He remained next to the window facing west and pretended to read Ambler.

'All ok?' Erna asked.

'All perfect. And you?'

'Me, too. Quite a stretch to Samedan and back. You notice that you're no longer twenty.'

After her bath, she joined him, pens and a heap of post cards at the ready.

'I must write a few, at last.'

She sat down, face towards her father. There were the binoculars.

'Have you seen any ibex?'

'Not a single one.'

'Admit it: you didn't even look.'

'Of course I did. For a long time, in fact. But there was nothing to see. The weather was clearly too ghastly for ibex.'

He kept silent, both about his observation as well as his phone investigations. He feared her indulgent smile, not wanting her to get the impression that he had lost the plot.

He watched his daughter as she, head slightly tilted, wrote picture postcards to friends and family. To think that she was forty-six, unmarried, and still lived with him. She had had a few relationships, the first before she was twenty. But in his view, there had been nobody who would have been husband material. His wife, who died fifteen years ago, had not always seen eye to eye with him in this respect.

'No sooner has the girl met a man, than you make a judgement. At least give the child a chance to get some experience.'

He had considered this irresponsible chitchat and did not hold back in saying so.

Now that he looked at his daughter's face, as it had grown older, he asked himself if his wife had not, after all, been right. Was there not a shadow of disappointment on this forehead, in these eyes, around this mouth? Since his wife's death, Erna had never spoken of wedding plans again, nor seemed to have had further serious relationships. They had both got used to the unspoken thought that Erna would stay with him.

'What do you think?' Erna lifted her head.

'Oh, nothing important', he said. 'Are you skiing again tomorrow?'

'No, I have agreed to meet the Rosenthals again. Caflisch has another day off.'

At seven o'clock on the dot, they took the elevator down for dinner. Mrs Bär sat in the foyer and wanted to know if he had seen ibex. No, he said, despite having looked very hard.

'There is time. You are not leaving so soon, after all.'

'Only in five days', Vontobel replied.

'Keep the binoculars until then. The ibex will surely make an appearance.'

He thanked her and was glad that she would let him keep them. If she had wanted to have them back, he would even have asked to be allowed to use them again, at least tomorrow.

After dinner, which had as usual been excellent, Mrs Rosenthal joined them at their table.

'I really have to congratulate you on your daughter, Mr Vontobel. Not only does she look after her father selflessly, she is, in addition, a fantastic cross-country skier. Left us all far behind today.'

He nodded and was proud of Erna. The man below the rocks slowly disappeared in the soothing fog, which the Valtellina had laid across his brain.

A buffet had been arranged in the foyer, and when Vontobel and Erna came out of the dining room, the first guests were arriving.

The community were giving a reception for one of their citizens, who had been elected to parliament in Berne, it was said. Vontobel saw Mrs Bär stand next to a strongly built man who looked a bit like a farmer. She spotted Vontobel and called: 'I know you do not believe me, but here you see the man who is the expert on ibex. May I introduce Mr Giovanelli, the officer in charge of hunting up here, so-to-speak the father of all ibex.'

Was he the man he had seen below the rocks? Vontobel could not say. But it must be easy to find out. He only had to be careful. He was aware how readily people made fun of old men.

'Do you actually know how many ibex there are in the rocks over there?' he asked.

'Around thirty, at a guess', the gamekeeper retorted in his guttural dialect.

'And you count them?'

'Yes, occasionally one would go up there to check.'

'In winter, too?' Vontobel inched towards the crux of the matter.

'There are fewer in winter.'

'And in weather like today?'

'Certainly not', Giovanelli said, and added that he had been in Fextal that day.

Now Vontobel knew what he had wanted to know.

The man with the gun had not been the gamekeeper. But if it had not been the gamekeeper, then there only remained a poacher. Vontobel could hardly suppress the joy that rose in him. He had observed a poacher plying his illegal trade.

He wondered whether he should make a comment. But that might look as if he was showing off, so he preferred to remain silent.

That night he could not sleep. He was excited and it felt to him as if, after all these years, his holidays had a purpose at last. Would he, actually, still have gone to the Engadin if Erna had not insisted, claiming it was good for his health? Hardly. But now he had got onto a poacher. The binoculars were on hand for tomorrow, near the window. Vontobel would be busy all day.

He waited nervously until Erna left again with the Rosenthals. The weather was like yesterday, gloomy and overcast, snow falling, the peaks concealed in the clouds. Vontobel shifted the chair to the most advantageous position, pushed the table closer so that it was within reach and put out Ambler, in case there was a long wait. He looked outside. Still too dark. For the time being, it was Ambler's turn.

Towards noon, the skies brightened up somewhat. Vontobel took the binoculars; the search started. He let his eyes wander systematically across the snow fields, over the rocks, along the edges of the forest, between the individual, lone pine trees. Despite the weather, visibility was not bad. Vontobel recognised trails. No skiing tracks, but tracks of animals, a whole lot of them. And then he saw, protected by a rock, the animals, a whole herd of ibex. He counted. There had to be at least a dozen.

A mere twenty-four hours earlier, the animals would have been of no interest to him. For so many years, he had not seen any ibex. Why now? He could have looked it up in a dictionary. Surely, there would have been a picture. Those were his thoughts yesterday. Today, all this had changed. As if electrified, he followed every move of the herd. Breathlessly, he twiddled with the binoculars and kept his eyes glued to the animals.

The same was the case for someone else. Vontobel saw him only after a few minutes. He stood motionless on a rocky ledge, about one hundred metres further to the right, above the animals. The poacher.

He had put the skis behind him in the snow. The hunting rifle was hanging across his back. He stood, as if he were a piece of rock himself, black in front of the snowy white and he observed the ibex, just as Vontobel was now observing him. Vontobel felt the tension through the binoculars. The chap over there was a captive, a prisoner of the ibex, shackled and damned to stand on that stone and wait. Their yellow eyes had entranced him. Vontobel thought he had read that ibex had yellow eyes with a horizontal black line.

Vontobel's eyes returned to the ibex. The herd shifted slowly to the left. Their horns bobbed up and down ponderously with each step. There was a headwind: they could not smell the enemy, close as he was. But Vontobel could see him. The movement of the animals had caused the poacher to move, as if they were connected by threads. He left his skis in the snow. He followed equally slowly, at a safe distance. But it only seemed like this. Vontobel quickly recognised the ploy.

The poacher wanted to go around the ibex at the level above them, in order to wait for them afterwards, protected by a big rock. He wanted them to parade directly into the muzzle of his gun.

Vontobel would now, for his part, have loved to have a gun, to warn the animals and ensure that the poacher failed. Did he really want this? Was he now trembling for the animals or was he waiting for the shot?

In the meantime, the man had taken the rifle from his shoulder and held it, ready to shoot, on his knees.

The animals approached the rock unsuspecting. Vontobel was panting like a hunting dog behind his binoculars. He barely dared look from the animals to the hunter and back, for fear of chasing away the ibex.

The poacher lifted the gun to his left cheek. Left-handed, Vontobel noted.

The first ibex strode towards him with a straight back. The shot rang out. Vontobel did not hear it. But he noticed it from the rifle of the gunman and the animal. The other ibex stood motionless, then they turned and raced away upwards. The first had jumped up and collapsed. The poacher got up and climbed down to the animal that had been hit. He took it by the horns, like a sledge, and dragged it into the shelter of the pine trees below. But Vontobel kept watching him. He was spellbound to watch how the poacher bundled the shot animal into a parcel in the shade of the pine trees. He observed how he went up to get his skis and how he skied down into the valley with the dead ibex.

He lost him when he was in the lower, denser forest. He put the binoculars on the table and only then noticed that he had forgotten to drink the bubbles he drank every lunch time.

Vontobel looked at his watch. It was nearly two o'clock. What should he do now? Call the police? He had, admittedly, seen everything clearly enough through the binoculars, but would they believe him? He had heard too much about the strong bond among the locals. Soon Erna would return. Should he tell her about it?

She surprised him as he closed the champagne bottle again. He told her, and she listened, while painting her nails.

'You have got to call the police', she said, after having heard to the whole story. 'It's your duty.'

He still hesitated.

After her nails were dry, Erna went back to writing post cards. 'Don't you want to ring?' she asked.

He could not make up his mind.

Later on, she said she'd take the cards to the post office and when she returned, she told him that she had seen the policeman. He would come round during the evening. And then she had looked up Caflisch, her skiing teacher, to invite him to a long overdue dinner again.

They were already seated, Vontobel and Erna, and waiting for the skiing teacher. When he entered, Vontobel knew that he was the poacher. His size, the way he moved – everything fitted.

Erna showed herself, shy but cheerful. Vontobel was lying in ambush just like the poacher in the afternoon. He observed the man who sat opposite him.

'My father has made an exciting discovery today', Erna said. 'He has observed a poacher in flagrante.'

Did the skiing teacher flinch? Vontobel was not sure.

Caflisch asked: 'And — did you recognise the man?'

As Vontobel said he had not; the subject appeared not to interest him anymore.

Over coffee, the skiing teacher and Erna agreed the lessons for the next few days. He pulled a small diary out and noted dates and times. He wrote with his left hand.

The skiing teacher took leave quite early, explaining that he had had an exhausting day. Erna seemed to be sorry. She stayed in the foyer with her father, in order to wait for the policeman.

'Your daughter told me that you had observed a poacher, Your Honour.'

Vontobel beamed at the policeman.

'Yes, and I can also tell you who it is. The man who left the hotel five minutes ago. Skiing teacher Caflisch, who lives next door. I can definitely identify him.'

Erna emitted a little cry of horror.

'This has been long my suspicion', the policeman said. 'Let's in that case pay him a visit.'

'I'll join you', Erna called.

'If you like', the policeman said.

Vontobel stayed on his own and gazed after the two. At that moment, Mrs Bär approached him.

'You entertained your daughter's skiing teacher? I believe I owe it to you, Mr Vontobel, to tell you the rumours about him. Your daughter is supposed to, and not only since yesterday, have . . . with Caflisch, who lives over there with his mother, unmarried, so she is supposed to —'

For years, Erna had insisted coming here for three weeks. Every year she repeated how good this was for him, and she always booked ahead, without asking him, for the next year.

Suddenly he heard a commotion and saw his daughter rushing up to him. Her eyes were yellow with hatred, like the eyes of the ibex. He noticed that she held the hunting rifle, aimed at him, and now he heard the shot.

Was he able to hear it?

His Lordship

It was one of these dazzling February days, with a brightness you can only find in the Engadin. They slowly gnaw at your nerves and take away all your strength, as they do not allow you to sleep at night.

We set out shortly before noon, took the postbus to Sils Maria and walked from there across the frozen lake to Maloja to have a little something to eat; but then we were too tired to return on foot and therefore took the postbus again and were already back in the hotel around three o'clock.

Before we got up to our room, we had a drink at the bar. Around this time of day there was normally nobody in the foyer and the stools stood without purpose by the bar. All guests were outside in the sun and snow.

On this day, however, a Sunday, a single, elderly gentleman sat there, on his own. He drank a beer, smoked a very thin cigarillo in an amber holder and wrote a postcard. This seemed to cause him trouble. He was more lying than sitting at the bar, as he was writing. Each time the waiter appeared behind him, the man talked to him in Italian. The guest was dressed unobtrusively, but expensively; camel hair jacket with shirt and tie, with a dark blue loden coat, which he did not take off despite the warm temperature in the foyer. He had thick glasses. When the waiter went away, the man bent over his postcard, read what he had written in the way short-sighted people do, and continued to write.

The gin and tonic had not quenched our thirst; we wanted to order a beer, as well. I went to the bar. As the waiter was slow in turning up, I fell into conversation with the card-writer, and was immediately struck with his refined Italian and impeccable manners. He said: 'The weather is as beautiful as it was a week ago. I was also here then. In the winter, I come up here every Sunday, if possible, to escape the smog in Milan.'

His face was red from the sun. He, too, ordered another beer. The waiter addressed him with 'Your Lordship'.

'On days like today, you understand that Nietzsche was attracted to this region as if by a magnet and yet he could not remain here. I sympathise. Our eyes and our brain can hardly tolerate this glare.'

'There is supposed to be a real Nietzsche revival in Italy', I said.

'Yes', the man replied, 'he certainly has a strong influence on contemporary philosophy. Think of Vattimo and others; Vattimo is merely the best-known. He is famous not least because the publishers of the critical edition of Vattimo's complete works are also Italian.'

In the meantime my wife had joined us. Our beers had arrived and been drunk, and I signed for them with room number and name. We wished the card-writer a good day and took the lift to our room.

There was not a single evening when we did not read the *Bündner Tagblatt*, the local daily. Three days later, on Wednesday, we read that there was a killer on the loose in Milan. During the night from Saturday to Sunday, another young woman had been murdered on her return from a party, the same way three others had been killed before, namely strangled with bare hands. And each time the relatives received a picture postcard from the Engadin a few days later, with a punctilious description of the circumstances and sent on Sunday. Nina read the article to me, in the way one reads short newspaper articles to each other on holiday.

'Fits our man from Sunday at the bar exactly', she said and laughed.

The blindingly bright weather continued for the whole week. The following Sunday we hiked through the woods all the way to Pontresina. Having worked up an appetite, we decided to stop off for a bite to eat. We found an empty table and ordered. When we had finished eating, Nina nudged me.

'Turn around, but quietly. Behind you, in the corner. The killer from Milan.'

There was His Lordship who wrote, bent low over the table, a picture postcard, drank a beer and smoked a thin cigarillo, the yellow amber tip of the holder in his hand. Despite my caution, he noticed us. He came over, sat on the free chair, not without having asked us, particularly Nina, for permission to do so.

'Didn't you say you had studied in Basel?'

'Yes.'

'In that case you will no doubt know — you remember we talked about Nietzsche a week ago — how Professor Overbeck from Basel fetched his friend home in 1889 after Nietzsche had become insane in Torino and had written cards to Overbeck and also to Jacob Burckhardt, which he signed "Antichrist" or "The crucified".'

'That man Overbeck', I replied, 'was a professor of theology, but insisted, that he personally was not a Christian, indeed, that he could not be a Christian.'

'An interesting man. I read his book about "Christianity of Theology" some time ago', His Lordship declared.

I was impressed.

'And you — are you writing cards like Nietzsche?' Nina asked.

His Lordship looked at her.

'A big word — calmly spoken, Signora', he retorted, and bid us goodbye.

'After all the killer', Nina laughed, as we passed Stazersee on our way home.

In the hotel we told the waiter at the bar that we had encountered His Lordship in Pontresina.

'Yes, a very friendly man, very classy and very sophisticated', the waiter said.

'He wrote a postcard. Like last Sunday.'

'Every time he is here he writes a postcard', the waiter replied.

'Just like that killer from Milan', said Nina.

The waiter then told us that his Italian Sunday paper had again reported on a murder.

'Well, perhaps our man after all', Nina interjected.

'You're not serious, Signora', the waiter said. 'Such a gallant gentleman, so polite and so highly educated. Out of the question.'

We downed our glasses; I signed the chit. Somehow relieved, we went to the lift and went upstairs to change for dinner.

We gave up our habit of reading the *Bündner Tagblatt* every night during those holidays.

Miss Stamps wants to be left alone

Everyone in the hotel knew that Miss Stamps, who every year between the second and the last week of February occupied the most expensive suite — the one with views on Lake Sils and Piz Margna — was in reality Angela Lightington, the author of a dozen or more crime stories, which were among the best in the genre. One knew Miss Lightington; her photograph could, after all, be seen on the back cover of each of her books. They were all available from the nearby library, congenially translated by Henriette Kiechlhuber. But nobody in the hotel was reading one of Angela Lightington's novels, at least not in public, and much less did anyone talk to Miss Stamps, neither under her real name nor under her vacation-induced *nom de plume*. As if a matter of course, a mantle of discretion had wrapped itself around this single lady of a certain age, in which she huddled herself up and which obviously made her feel very comfy.

When one evening in February two years ago, a cheeky young mother of two, who had already made a spectacle of herself in the dining room with her piercing voice, steered towards Miss Stamps, book in hand — just as the author was dissecting a king prawn from the grill — and asked her for an autograph, loud enough to be heard by all. This was felt to be an outrageous breach of protocol and it was commented on in terms of shock and dismay by the guests chatting in the foyer after dinner.

The following year, the woman and her family were informed, with regret, when they enquired about availability, that the hotel was completely booked out for the whole winter season. Miss Stamps expressed her gratitude to the director as soon as she arrived.

'We do what we can for our guests', he nodded.

Dinner was served from 7 o'clock. Miss Stamps took the lift down at ten past. She did not like to eat late. Signor Bruno, chef de service, accompanied her to her table. As happened every year, the table in the back corner on the left was reserved for her. From here she saw everyone and hardly anyone saw her. Only a few people were dining at this time. Some distance from her, the old couple; he an emeritus professor in the history of theology at a German university who talked incessantly. The two were always here for a fortnight. Then, there was a lonely younger man whom Miss Stamps had never seen and a couple, both around sixty, nearest to her, whom she did not know either. The man had a red face and spooned his soup with his elbows on the table.

'High blood pressure and bad upbringing', Miss Stamps thought to herself.

She chose fish for her second course and ordered, in addition to the Valtellina, which she normally drank, a bottle of white from the Vaud.

'I hope the chef is the same', she said to the waiter in her broken and very English-sounding Italian.

The waiter nodded reassuringly.

'Nothing ever changes around here. Neither the guests, nor the cooks.'

Miss Stamps, normally very reserved and a bit stiff, laughed, rubbed her hands in an exaggerated way, and observed the young couple who were entering the dining room.

The white was poured. She savoured its refreshing bouquet. The first course, the bouillon, had been delicious and now Miss Stamps was looking forward to the fish. Precisely when the waiter served it, dull white on the dark green spinach leaves, the drama started.

The man, whose poor table manners had caught her eye, complained to the waiter about the salad, as far as Miss Stamps could understand. He became louder with every sentence, forcing Miss Stamps to listen. He was not prepared to pay such a price for this food. Then he increased the noise level further. The soup consisted of meat from the day before yesterday, the tiny amount of fish was so small that it could only be found with the help of a magnifying glass, and now this limp stuff. The meat, he claimed, had been served only lukewarm yesterday and today he was expected to put up with wilting green fodder. If it continued in this way —

The waiter tried, attentively but unsuccessfully, to calm the man, whose face turn increasingly red. He did not allow anyone to get a word in edgeways, not even his wife. He pushed her hand away; the waiter stood next to him with a stiff back and a dull face, as if he were deaf.

The man's face was now dark red, then changed to blue, and words like 'fraud', 'rip-off', 'racket' and 'abysmal fodder' emerged from his distorted mouth.

Suddenly he choked. He began to cough violently. The waiter grabbed the opportunity to beat a hasty retreat.

The woman got up and smacked him with the flat of her hand as he was gasping for air till the coughing subsided.

No sooner had it passed than the man continued his rant, albeit less noisily — Miss Stamps did not understand the details any more. . . but in a continuous stream, which only petered out when the couple had finished their meal and got up.

Miss Stamps' knife, with which she cut her rack of lamb, trembled slightly, and because she did not want to wait for the sommelier to pour her more wine, she spilt some over the tablecloth. The meal had been spoilt for her. How she feared and loathed such scenes! She could not sit there like others, detached from it all, without feeling personally upset.

She gulped down dessert in a rush and then got up. She would have loved to sit in the foyer for a while to smoke a cigarette, but when she saw that the man and his wife had settled down at a little table for smokers, she refrained. She knew that she would not be able to stop herself listening intently, afraid the torrent of words would start again.

Miss Stamps never slept well during the first night: this had to do with the stimulating climate and the altitude. This time, however, she did not close an eye. The unpleasant person with the red head and the noise he made when he talked did not allow her any peace. She would have loved nothing more than to get up in the middle of the night and run away. She felt trapped.

Next morning, at breakfast, she did not see the man and his wife. Who knows, perhaps they had left. If not, then he must have had a bad day yesterday and had now returned to being a civilised human being. Miss Stamps berated herself for being so touchy and called herself a 'hysterical goose'. She had to laugh about herself.

It was a glorious day. At eleven, she started for a three-hour hike over the frozen lake to Maloja and back. Then she slept till about five, and after that she wrote. These were her first, loose thoughts towards a new novel, whose shape did not yet want to emerge. Next, she ran a bath and enjoyed the hot water. Her rumbling stomach reminded her that she had not eaten since breakfast.

She went down in a new dress with a colourful scarf around her neck and white cuffs. Next to her, the man and his wife were already seated, he with his elbows on the table tearing sullenly at something unrecognisable with his fork. She heard his bleating ramblings from afar. He moaned, head dark red, about the food, the service, the hotel.

Twice, the woman said: 'Think of your blood pressure, Willy.'

He did not stop. The waiter approached him as if he were an unlocked grenade and, his upper body slightly averted, pushed the plate towards him. Willy pointed at it with his finger and ranted before he had even tasted it.

Miss Stamps ate without joy, although the main course was sautéed poularde, one of her particular favourites. In her agitation she had drunk a bit too much Valtellina, as she noticed when she left. She did not want to sit down in the foyer, but immediately took the lift upstairs. During the night, her digestive system caused her problems: she was suffering from a stomach ache.

In the morning, she could no longer suppress the thought of the man whose wife called him Willy. Already under the shower he started to bother her and by the time she was dressed, Willy was a bogeyman who ruined her holidays and against whom she was defenceless. Although Willy and his wife were again not at breakfast, they were there, as far as Miss Stamps was concerned. On her midday walk through the sunshine, she could not shake off her troublesome companions either. Willy was omnipresent, with his crimson head and his endless moaning.

Miss Stamps did not feel like working after her stroll. To relax, she soaked in her bath for nearly an hour. Should she simply go down to dinner later? That would have turned her day's schedule upside down and she knew what consequences that had on her work. She might as well leave.

Dinner proceeded as it had done on the previous evening. When Willy ordered a new bottle of wine, thunder and lightning descended over the poor waiter as they had done during Noah's Flood. Everything was mentioned: the thin soup, the minute portion of fish, the lukewarm meat, the excessive cost of the drinks, the cold wine. Only with difficulty did Miss Stamps manage to finish her meal. And no good night's sleep yet again, thanks to Willy.

Next morning, the third of her holiday, she addressed the director after breakfast and enquired who the swearing guest was and whether it was not possible to throw him out. The director asked her into his office and revealed to her, amid gestures of despair, that he was an influential member of the board of the hotel's own bank.

'You can imagine, my dear Miss Stamps, that we therefore have to be particularly careful. But I can reassure you we shall do our utmost.'

'I'd be most grateful', Miss Stamps replied, without having any illusions. She realised that she had to help herself.

Fearing the power of money, nobody would even lift a finger.

She had lots of time to think about it during her long, sunny walk. Abandon her holiday? Out of the question. She would reproach herself for months if she fled the red-headed monster. Unless she wanted to endanger her writing project, she must not give in.

She thought of Ernest, the hero of her last five novels. What would Ernest do in her situation? What a question! He'd kill him.

Around three o'clock, Miss Stamps returned to the hotel, having come to a decision. The only question was how to put it into practice. Ernest always found an infallible solution.

As early as that evening, a coincidence came to her aid. She was a bit earlier than usual in the dining room and saw how Willy took his pills before the meal. He shook a few tablets from a small dark-brown chemist's bottle into his hand and tossed them with a sweep into his mouth, which was contorted with disgust. The little bottle stood next to Willy's napkin. Willy and his wife left it there when they got up and Miss Stamps could check discreetly what the label said. Something against high blood pressure, she assumed. She made a mental note of the name.

As it happened, Willy had been quite bearable during the day, she said to herself when she was back in the lift. He had, admittedly, still grumbled as usual, but unlike on the other evenings, it had not got under her skin so much. Miss Stamps did not fool herself. She knew the reason.

It was not yet ten o'clock and therefore perfectly in order for her to call a friend, a doctor in Lugano.

'I am in the Engadin with a friend, Doctor. She is suffering from low blood pressure. What should she take? No, it would certainly have to be something strong. What is the name? I'll write it down. Yes, yes, I understand, only under doctor's orders, of course. We'll go to a doctor tomorrow, but you know, it is a local village surgery. Thus, my call to you first. Don't worry. Thank you, Doctor, thank you so much, and please give my regards to your wife. Yes, the weather is fantastic.'

Now there was the matter of getting the medicine. Going to the pharmacy without a prescription was not possible. Miss Stamps looked at her watch again. She would have to be patient until tomorrow.

She telephoned even before her shower. Her Swiss publisher was already in his office and she moaned as dramatically as she could that she had left her blood pressure drugs in London.

'Without my tablets I cannot live, let alone write. I fall asleep standing up. And, worse than that, I don't have the prescription with me either.'

No problem, the publisher reassured her; there were enough doctors among his friends. Before midday a prescription was faxed, issued by a specialist in internal medicine in Zurich.

There was not sufficient time to deal with everything on that day, as Miss Stamps wanted to buy the medication away from Sils.

Dinner was, again, illuminating for her. 48 hours before, she would have found it unbearable, but since her decision, she followed Willy's outbursts with a certain amount of sympathy, even. She now observed the man with the cool interest of an entomologist. Willy complained again loudly, got worked up, so that his head turned red first, blue thereafter. And then — and this was new — he broke down. He collapsed on his chair, panted and looked as if he was dead. The chef de service brought ice cubes, Willy's wife grabbed the little brown bottle of drugs and stuffed a few pills into Willy's mouth.

Five minutes later, Willy had recovered sufficiently to be able to get up and for his wife to lead him from the dining room. Miss Stamps kept a close watch and her observant eyes did not miss the glance Willy's wife gave the chef de service.

After breakfast the next morning, Miss Stamps went to Zuoz on hired cross-country skis. A considerable effort, but the end justifies the means. In the pharmacy she handed in the prescription and received a pack of 25 pills without the slightest problem. The pharmacist drew her attention to the need for medical control, especially at this altitude.

In a jolly mood, Miss Stamps took the Rhätische Bahn back to St Moritz and took a taxi from there to Sils. Shortly after four o'clock, she was back in her room.

She made meticulous preparations. She dressed festively; today was Friday, the day of the farmers' buffet. There was a coming and going in the dining hall like never before. She went down earlier than usual.

In the dining room, nobody was yet to be seen other than cooks and waiters who were arranging the buffet. Miss Stamps pretended to look for something, snatched Willy's medication, which was on the table next to hers, opened it and emptied her paper bag full of pills into it. Then she left again and read an old edition of *The Times* in the foyer.

When Miss Stamps returned to the dining hall, Willy and his wife were already there and eating. Willy's wife seemed not to enjoy her food. Her face appeared tired and ill. On the other hand, Willy had a good day. He announced, so that everyone could hear it, that he wished the food was like this every night; at last he had something decent between his teeth.

Then — Miss Stamps was in the process of helping herself to some corn salad from the buffet — Willy was served dessert. Fresh strawberries with cream. No sooner had Willy put the first strawberry, a winter strawberry, to his mouth than he exploded like a grenade. He spat out the slightly chewed berry in a high arc, swore like a hangman's assistant and could not stop himself even after a half dozen sentences. His head turned red and then, finally, blue. After that, he sank back into his chair and fell silent.

His wife looked at him with wide open eyes. There is no terror in this, Miss Stamps thought. Willy's wife hesitated for a moment, took the little bottle and shoved pills between her husband's lips. He swallowed. He groaned. Then his head fell back. Willy was dead.

The doctor arrived quickly. He confirmed the man's passing. Willy's excitement was reported to him and he tasted, purely as a routine, one of the strawberries from Willy's plate. He spat it out at once.

'Ah, that's foul, what have you put on this?' he called out.

The chef, standing in the door frame, giggled, the chef de service nodded and — as Miss Stamps clearly saw — gave Willy's wife a conspiratorial look. The glance he got in return was full of gratitude.

'I think it's only the cream. A bit rancid', she said, quietly.

The doctor looked at the dead man once more. Then he grasped the little brown bottle, unscrewed it and inspected one of the pills. The policeman and the director stepped towards him. The doctor pointed to the pill on his palm while talking. The director looked questioningly over to Miss Stamps. How could you! Were we not just about sorting out this case, she read in his eyes. The doctor and the policeman went to her table together.

'Miss Stamps?' the doctor asked.

She nodded.

'Miss Stamps, I would have visited you tomorrow. A colleague from university, a specialist in Zurich, called me today. He was concerned because he prescribed a drug for you without knowing you. A very strong drug. He thought you should not take it without seeing a doctor.'

'Mrs Lightington', the policeman said, 'I believe you owe us an explanation.'

'Camillo's secret'

The bar is worth seeing. The back wall consists of two circular arches, like the little toy weather boxes of my childhood. When the weather is good, the colourfully dressed young girl puppet emerges from the left; when the weather is bad, the little man, dressed in black and white, emerges from the right. Above the two arches there is a shelf across the width of the wall, on which Camillo's trophies are.

Camillo is the bartender. He has been working in the hotel at least as long as we have come here for our winter holidays. A small, wiry Italian with a big mouth. His sayings are legendary and deserve to be. His creations deserve it even more. They have fanciful names, 'Bloody Mary' or 'Sunshine', 'Saratoga', 'La Margna' and so on. Most have a reddish colour and are served with slices of orange on the rim of the glass and with colourful straws. On the menu of the bar, Camillo's creations are all listed. Underneath each name there is information on where it was first mixed and what prize he had won with it. For example, 'Lady's Dream', St Moritz 1976. Or 'Whisky Pizz Err', Nice 1982. For each prized position Camillo had reached with one of his drinks, there is a cup.

Yesterday, after dinner, I sat in the foyer and had Camillo's assembled awards in front of me. While I was drinking my usual good-night-beer, I counted them. There were 38. Thirty-eight trophies, prize cups and goblets of all possible shapes.

Then my attention was drawn to the architect. The 'architect' is an elderly (from my point of view elderly) gentleman who in the evening usually wears a red jacket and a colourful shirt with a quaintly patterned tie. He is tall and relatively heavy set, with short cropped hair. Accompanied by a strikingly beautiful young woman, possibly his wife. Every night, the two of them first drink a glass of champagne, then she has a brandy and he has the drink of the day, whose name is . written down at the entrance to the bar.

The architect appears to know Camillo well, and Camillo books the same table for him and his lady companion every evening. They joke and laugh, and the architect calls Camillo 'maestro'. Camillo calls the architect 'professore'.

Last night, however, after the architect had drunk the champagne with his wife just like every evening, and after the waiter had served her the brandy, and Camillo had personally brought him the drink of the day — it was called 'Sunshine' — and the architect had tasted some of it, there was a disturbance at the table. The architect called Camillo back. He pointed angrily at the glass with the reddish drink. I could not understand what he said, but it must have been a tetchy complaint, because Camillo threw himself into the posture of an offended rooster. The architect became increasingly loud.

'Impossible, professore, totally out of the question', Camillo protested.

'I insist; it does taste disgusting!' the architect retorted.

At that, the barkeeper furiously grabbed the glass. It looked as if he wanted to hurl it at the architect's face.

'You are offending me', he said sharply, walked off with long strides and disappeared through an arch in the bar.

Not long thereafter he returned smiling. On a silver tablet, he served the architect a new drink. The architect took a sip.

'You see', he said satisfied.

Camillo laughed out loud. 'It's the same glass. I have only filled it up a bit, professore', he said, as he departed.

'One should take away all your prize cups, Camillo', shouted the architect, half joking, after him.

I finished my beer and went to bed, falling asleep quickly. In the morning, I woke up earlier than usual. As I could not go back to sleep, I got up and dressed warmly to go outside for a few minutes. I have learnt that I then tend to continue to sleep all the better afterwards.

The foyer was brightly lit. Without taking any further notice of this, I left the house. The cold air filled my lungs and calmed my nerves.

When I returned after ten minutes, a black car was in front of the entrance, the hatchback open. Two men were in the process of sliding a metal coffin into the car on a rail. The hotel director, hauled out of bed, stood by. When he saw me, he looked at me in a grumpy way.

'What's up?'

'We have a death. Please, don't tell a soul. A death in the hotel can have really unpleasant consequences.'

'Who is it, then?'

109

There was no need for him to answer. The same moment the architect's wife came out of the house and got into the hearse weeping. I went upstairs and back into bed.

It probably has not become public knowledge. At least, nobody let on. And it's pure coincidence that I am sitting at the same table as yesterday for my good-night-beer, with a good view towards the trophies.

Camillo stalks about with his head carried high. I cannot stop myself counting his prize cups again. 39. One more than yesterday. Is it the elegant narrow one on the left?

I glance over to the entrance to see what drink of the day is announced there. 'Camillo's Secret'. I take the card on the table. At the bottom there is a handwritten addition: 'Camillo's Secret'.

The passenger

To see someone standing with skis at the roadside trying to hitch a lift surprised Burkard Lehmann, a 68-year-old retired secondary school teacher who was on his way to the Engadin in his new four-wheel drive Subaru. The girl had attached the cross-country ski straps both sides of her rucksack, and it looked as if she had two wings. An angel, thought Burkard, and stopped. He was a short distance above Bivio on the road towards the Julier Pass.

'Where do you want to go?' Burkard asked.

'Where are you driving to?'

'I'm going to the Engadin, to Sils Maria', Burkard replied.

'In that case, I'll go to the Engadin, too', the girl said. 'May I come with you?'

Burkard got out, helped her detach the skis from the rucksack and clipped them onto the roof rack, where his own skis were. He put the rucksack, small and light as it was, on the back seat.

He liked the girl. Her bouncing movements, the little round face under the short black woolly hair, the colourful skiing outfit; it all appealed to him. There was a breath of fresh air around the girl, and Burkard sucked it up.

The girl sat next to him. Even while sitting, there was a bounce in her. Burkard found it delightful.

'You don't have a specific destination?' he asked as he drove on.

'I go wherever I am taken.'

'And where do you come from?'

'Oh, from the Unterland'[4]

That was not a very precise place name, and although Burkard was regarded a dialect expert, he could not make out a specific characteristic in her language. Even so, he did not delve more deeply. He thought it charming not to know everything.

'And you?' the girl asked.

'My name is Burkard Lehmann, I'm sixty-eight, a retired secondary-school teacher from Zurich and I'm on my way to Sils Maria for a fortnight.'

Why did he not want to know anything specific about the girl and why did he feel the urge to tell her as much as possible about himself? Ten minutes later, he still knew nothing about his passenger, as if the girl had no history, but she knew nearly everything about him. For example, that he would have loved to continue studying history until graduation, but that this had not been possible for financial reasons.

He was twenty-six when he got married. He had met Verena, his wife, in the teacher training college and it had been clear, even then, that for her there would never be another man and that for him there would never be another woman. And this was, indeed, how it turned out to be.

---

[4] 'Unterland' is the term for the lower-lying regions in the northern part of Switzerland, where there are no mountains.

They were engaged for eight years and, after he had passed the secondary teaching diploma, they got married.

The plan had been that Verena would work until they had children, but when none arrived, she continued teaching, even when they moved into the city. They were lucky enough to be able to work in the same building, even in town, and discussed everything that happened at school, as well as everything else in life. They travelled to work together every day; this was particularly important for them. And then, of course, they always spent the holidays together. For the last twenty years, they had gone to Sils for a fortnight every winter. They always stayed in the same hotel, which was very conveniently located for cross-country skiing. Every time they had the same room, which was very quiet, on the top floor.

In the first few years, they still went on downhill pistes, but after that, they increasingly changed to cross-country skiing until, ten years ago, when they gave up alpine skiing altogether.

Year after year, they were looking forward to the next holidays until, roughly two-and-a-half years ago, Verena, by then also retired, fell seriously ill from one day to the next, suddenly, out of the blue. Pancreatic cancer. Admittedly, they managed to travel to the Engadin once more, despite her illness. Indeed, both even stood on their cross-country skis again and did their little rounds. They were encouraged and hoped that there might, perhaps, be an improvement. No sooner had they returned from their holidays, however, than it got worse and worse, ending in a rapid collapse, and Verena died at the end of May after many weeks of suffering.

'It was a blessed release for her, if one may put it like that', Burkard turned to his passenger.

But it had been hard and nearly unbearable for him, he said. In any case, last February he did not have the heart to drive into the Engadin on his own, and he had not once touched his cross-country skis since then.

But now, he declared, he had gathered all his courage. Already in September he had phoned the hotel to make a booking and told them that he wanted to return this year, but only on the condition that he could have the same room. He had suggested that he would pay the rate for a double room, but with meals for one person only. He had not held out much hope that the hotel would approve his proposal as it was high season, after all. He was all the more surprised, he told her, that he had been given the old, familiar room. And now he found himself driving up there, alone for the first time, and a bit fearful.

The girl sat next to Burkard and listened, and while he talked, he absorbed her scent, which loosened his tongue just like sweet wine. They had already passed between the first stumps of the columns marking the Julier Pass, when Burkard said: 'You know so much about me now, and I don't even know your name. Will you, at least, tell me your name?'

'I'm Lilith', the girl responded.

'Nothing else?'

'Nothing else.'

114

'Lilith. Strange name. Not without a dark meaning', Burkard said.

'Really?' the girl asked.

'And what are you planning to do in the Engadin?'

The girl shrugged her shoulders.

'Cross-country skiing', Burkard noted.

'Yes', the girl said.

'And where?'

'Don't know yet.'

'Not booked anywhere?'

'No.'

'And no friends or acquaintances, who are expecting you?'

'None.'

Suddenly Burkard was struck by a thought. Here was a girl who was not expected by anyone, whose scent enchanted him, whose bouncing movements cheered him up and whose proximity made him chatty. There was this girl here, and down there, in Sils Maria, which would soon come into sight, a double room in the hotel was waiting for him, and he was on his own. How about if he arrived together with her, instead of alone? The fact that a widower of a year-and-a-half had found a girlfriend was nothing scurrilous.

There was, of course, no need for anyone to know that they had only just met each other, if one could indeed put it in such words. And the fact that the girl was so much younger than he was — she was surely not even in her mid-twenties — well, too bad. Perhaps some might find this ludicrous. Let them.

Burkard was determined to suggest to Lilith that she should live with him for ten days. He was searching for words to tell her without raising a suspicion of immoral intentions. There was not much time. Once they were in the valley, Lilith would soon have to get out.

'The room I booked is, as I said, a double. And I'm on my own. If you didn't mind, I'd love to let you share the room with me for the ten days. I'd pay of course.'

He feared her embarrassment or her indignation. But she said in a completely business-like way: 'That does not bother me.'

'Does this mean that you accept my offer?' he asked, relieved.

'Yes.'

'But you mustn't believe — '.

'I believe nothing. No fear, Burkard. Nice name, Burkard. Somehow medieval, and posh. Totally different from the names that are fashionable nowadays. May I call you Burkard?'

'Yes, please. Thank you, Lilith.'

In Silvaplana, he turned right. Ten minutes later, they had reached their destination.

'I'm not alone, after all. We are together', Burkard told the receptionist, as if it was the most normal thing in the world and the receptionist reacted accordingly.

The porter in the green apron carried their luggage upstairs ahead of them; Burkard's two suitcases and Lilith's tiny rucksack. He put everything into the room and Burkard gave him his five-franc tip as usual. The porter thanked him and then closed the door.

There they were, Lilith and Burkard, and looked at each other. Lilith smiled. She approached him, laid her hands on his shoulders and kissed him on both cheeks.

'Thank you', she said. 'May I take a bath?'

He nodded. He lifted the bigger of his two cases onto the bed and opened it. Lilith got undressed without being bothered by his presence.

'I'm in the bathroom', she called, skipped out of the room and left the door open.

He heard how she ran the bath and stepped into the tub. She splashed and whistled. He heard her movements as she washed herself. In the meantime, he unpacked his second case and put everything neatly into the wardrobe on the left, as he had always done. The wardrobe on the right had always been designated Verena's. Once he had stowed the empty suitcases away in the closet by the door, he settled himself into the armchair at the window and waited.

Lilith emerged from the bathroom, towel slung around her hips. He looked, without being shy, at her small breasts which, like the rest of the girl, constantly bounced, and at the line which ran up from her navel.

She unpacked her things. There was not much — practically nothing — that had found room in the small rucksack. Without asking, she put the stuff into the wardrobe that had been Verena's.

He would buy her suitable clothes. He thought with joy of how they would go shopping in the elegant stores in St Moritz to choose something for her. He was so excited that he had to breathe deeply and felt a slight pressure around his heart, which reminded him that he must not forget to take his pills. Before that, he put his washbag into the bathroom.

Lilith's toothbrush was already there, as well as a few tubes and tiny pots, a lipstick and a gigantic oversized pink comb.

'Does one change for dinner here?' Lilith asked.

'Yes, on the whole, one does', he called back gently.

She didn't have anything suitable to change into, after all.

He closed the door, went to the loo, washed his hands and immersed his face in water.

When he returned to the room, Lilith was already dressed. She wore a cheap, colourful, skimpy dress in which she looked breathtaking. Burkard swapped, without feeling embarrassed, the crumpled corduroys for the dark ones, changed shirts and put on a tie. He also put a hankie into the breast pocket of his dark blue blazer with the gold buttons.

118

'That looks good', Lilith commented.

'Let's go', Burkard said, with a hint of exuberance. They stood next to each other in front of the mirror.

'I think we need to sort something out before we continue. Surely we should drop formalities now: two people sharing a room and addressing each other as "Sie"[5] would be very odd.'

'Burkard', Lilith said, and kissed him on the lips.

The chef de service had a broad smile when he saw Burkard approach with the young girl. Smile on, Burkard thought and proceeded proudly to their table.

Lilith ate with relish and was clearly enjoying the local Valtellina, which Burkard had ordered.

'She also bounces while she eats and drinks', Burkard thought cheerfully, and watched the short black lock, which bobbed up and down on her brow.

They took their time. Burkard could have looked at her forever and would have forgotten to eat. They were nearly the last to leave the dining room. It was past ten o'clock.

'I'm rather tired', Lilith said.

'Then let's go up straightaway.'

---

[5] In the German part of Switzerland, it is traditional that adults normally address each other with the formal 'Sie' and last name, rather than the informal 'Du' and first name. Only when both parties agree to use first names and confirm this with a toast, are first names used.

Nevertheless, they drank a whisky in the foyer. Burkard saw some familiar faces from previous years, but everyone stayed back, be it because of embarrassment, or discretion, or disapproval.

Upstairs, Lilith turned the radio on and went into the bathroom. The maid had turned the bed down and put night towels on the beds. On Burkard's bed, his blue and white pyjamas had been artistically draped into a special shape. On Lilith's bed, there was nothing.

Lilith emerged, undressed, out of the bathroom and climbed naked under the covers.

When Burkard, too, was in bed and the light had been turned off, Lilith's naked arm came out from under the blanket like a snake. She ruffled his hair and said: 'Thank you for everything. Sleep well.'

He propped himself up, leant over to her, as he had always done with Verena, breathed in her scent and kissed her on the lips.

'Sleep well. Thank you.'

Despite her wishes, he could not sleep. His senses were wide awake. He tried to make out her profile against the nocturnal light. He remembered that he had forgotten to take his medication. Oh well, let pills be pills. He listened to Lilith's breathing, but could not hear anything. Hoping to fall asleep, he turned away from her. That made finding sleep even more impossible so he turned around again and just lay there, eyes open.

'Burkard'. There was a whisper from the other bed.

'Yes', he whispered equally quietly.

'Are you asleep?'

'No.'

'Nor am I.'

Long pause.

'Burkard.'

'Yes.'

'Are you comfortable?'

'Why?'

'Wouldn't it be better near me? Why don't you move over?'

Again, the snake of her arm came over to him, took his hand and put it on the no-man's land of Lilith's naked stomach. There it remained. The snake let it be. The hand lay like dead, at first, then it came to life. It began to tremble, and the tremble continued, up his arm and spread through Burkard's body, growing to a tremor. He felt as if he were caught in an avalanche, which tore him away, forcing him to lose all control. He threw the blankets away and rolled over to Lilith's bed. He caressed her and lay on top of her, his brain burning and melting to a very small lump of black cinders.

He remained with her throughout the night. In the morning, with snow and sun shining into the room, they did not want to separate. They missed breakfast, and when, shortly after noon, they finally went down for a late coffee, they were already dressed for the cross-country loipe.

Lilith was keen to go out. She glided ahead through the dazzling sunshine, as if she had just had a full night's deep sleep. Burkard followed. He felt a sense of liberating exhaustion inside him. At last, the iron yoke that Verena's death had placed on him had been lifted. At last, he had stepped out of the shadow of the prison of grief into the sun and the daylight.

The longer they skied, the freer Burkard breathed, and the broader his breast grew. When they returned, they undressed, made love and then had to hurry up so as not to be late for dinner.

They hardly slept. Burkard felt the stream of life flow into his body like water into a dried-out riverbed.

When they were on their way to Silvaplana over the frozen lake, Lilith ahead, he behind her, he suddenly emitted a shout of joy against the deep blue sky. It was as if the vast infinite sky was sinking into his heart. Then the sky turned dark, and Burkard saw Verena stand in front of the black background. She waved at him. Behind her, there was an angel and he knew that it was the angel of death, a sweet young angel. The angel had Lilith's face and, instead of wings, carried two cross-country skis attached to a minuscule rucksack on his back.

Burkard lay dead on the ice, arms outstretched.

'Weak heart', the doctor, who had been called by cross-country skiers, noted. And he added: 'This happens a lot

122

during the first days of vacation. By the way, are there any next of kin?'

'Wasn't there a young girl ahead of him?' a woman asked.

'I have not seen anyone', the man next to her said.

The shoes hurt

Halfway across the frozen lake from Sils Maria to Maloja, the new shoes began to hurt 'the other one'. This was the third day of the skiing holiday, deep blue sky, glaring sunshine reflected on the snow, and it was the first time that he felt it; a piercing pain on the inside of the ankle, first on the left foot, and soon afterwards on the right, as if a razorblade was pressed into the flesh.

Perhaps he had tightened his shoes too much, Freddy suggested. They stopped. Freddy bent down and loosened the laces, which made him lose his balance and topple into the snow. They laughed. Then he tied his shoes for him again.

It became obvious very quickly that this had been pointless. The second step already caused pain in the left foot; and the right was no better. On the contrary, the pain became increasingly worse. Freddy suggested that he should position his feet differently in his shoes. That was no use either. The pain got worse.

Freddy looked ahead. The path to Maloja stretched itself in front of them. Certainly another hour. He turned around and looked back. The way back was nearly as long. Walking on or returning? It would make no difference. Endless painful steps were in front of the other one — whichever direction they went in.

If they went ahead, they could take the PostBus[6] in Maloja. It stopped right outside their hotel.

---

[6] The traditional, yellow coaches are now run by a company called 'PostBus'.

Freddy remembered one of his mother's favourite sentences. 'Just don't think of it and it won't hurt any more', she used to say, when he ran to her crying, as a child.

His mother. This was the first time that he had gone on holiday without his mother. She had died last June. He had not actually lived with her, but very close to her. He had to hide the other one from her.

'Get yourself a wife, for god's sake', she had often told him.

He and the other one knew the significance of that exactly.

'Don't you dare do that to me', was what she actually meant.

'Just don't think of it, then it won't hurt any more', he said.

Nevertheless, the other one continued to whine, his ankles aching like hell, and he would not be able to take a single step tomorrow. Freddy imagined how bloodshot blisters would be forming on the other one's feet and how the calf muscles would be tensing up with cramp because of the constant pain. But they were not his feet and legs, and the other one was of no concern to him, as long as he walked. He could look at him the way one looks at a fly before squashing it, but with less emotion; the way one looks at an interesting stone one has found on the way.

'You really just shouldn't think of it', Freddy said, once again, and they strode on vigorously.

Once back in the hotel, he would take the other one's shoes and socks off and examine the result of the pressure on the ankle with clinical attention.

The other one must be feeling every step and the longer they walked on, the more every step filled Freddy with satisfaction. When the path over the ice was uneven, or when they even sank in a bit, the blades would press deeper into the other one's ankles, cut open the skin and lay bare the bone — white shining through the bloody red.

In Maloja, they ate a pan-fried trout. The other one cut out its dull eyes with his fork.

When they got up from their meal, the hellish fire erupted afresh in the other one. Freddy saw him double over. He laughed; the guffaw foamed like a waterfall. The other one reacted instantly: he did not want to be a weakling and was determined not to be ridiculed. So, he gritted his teeth and marched on. Indeed, he decided that it would seem effeminate to take the PostBus, and requested that they trudged the long way back across the lake.

Twice, the other one threatened to flag on the way. But apart from the fact that it was impossible to sit down on the wide expanse of the frozen lake, Freddy only had to laugh scornfully for the other one to pick himself up again.

It had already started to grow dark when they approached the village and the hotel. Freddy sensed that the other one was losing his strength, just like sand runs out of a sack full of holes. He staggered.

A lady who approached them from the other direction asked whether he was not feeling well. Freddy answered for him that it was going to be ok. He laughed, cracking the whip of mockery, and the other one walked on, though he really felt no longer able to do so.

In the room, Freddy undid the other one's shoelaces and loosened the shafts to free his feet from the clasps. Then he tore down the socks. He expected to see bloodshot feet, but neither were they bloody, nor were there any blisters around the ankles. On the left, a red mark; on the right, a red mark, nothing more. The other one could count himself lucky.

After dinner, they took a short stroll into the village. The other one had put on the softest shoes he owned. The ankles, caressed by lambskin, did not hurt any more. They had a whisky at the bar of the Hotel Arnika and let their feet dangle from the stools. Freddy saw how the barmaid's cleavage aroused the other one. A young woman asked if the seat next to the other one was free. They did not object to her sitting down, neither did they mind that she caringly enquired if the other one was alone on holiday. Freddy noticed that the other one was excited by the woman's proximity. He gave him an encouraging prod.

Later, Freddy watched as the other one opened the buckle of his belt in their room. The woman had not even been surprised that he had followed her. Perhaps it had been his presence that had bothered the other one. He failed, and had to put up with Freddy's mocking grin, in addition to the disappointed nagging of the girl.

Freddy saw how fury and despair gripped the other one and observed with the calmness of a scientist how the other one put his hands around the sneering girl's throat; how he squeezed.

Freddy asked the other one to get dressed and fasten the buckle of his belt. They left the house. Back in the hotel they drank another whisky from the fridge in their room.

Freddy slept deeply. In the morning, they left the house early, again in brilliant sunshine, in order to walk to Maloja. Freddy noticed with malicious joy that the other one's shoes were already cutting his ankles after a hundred metres.

'Just don't think of it', declaimed Freddy.

In Maloja, the police were waiting. Not his business, but the other one's.

'Just don't think of it', whispered Freddy encouragingly and marched bravely towards the two officers.

The ladies' friend

Because the Engadin is so beautiful and the hotel so good, we have been going to the same place for ten years every winter. The hotel is big enough that one does not know all the other guests on the second visit. All the same, some faces remain in the memory until the next time.

This also applied to the ladies' friend. An elderly gentleman, over seventy, of pleasant appearance with white hair and a velvety whisper voice, who looked after a lady every season — a different one each time. He preferred older women who had had a misfortune. In a hotel of that size, something happens to someone all the time.

In front of the hotel entrance, a short-sighted lady, who has recently undergone a hip operation, breaks her foot on the ice. She has to be transported to hospital, returns after a week and sits in the foyer all afternoon. The wire-haired dachshund of a portly lady from Munich gets a sudden attack of diarrhoea and dies after two days, suffering from horrible cramps, despite a visit to the vet. The widow of an industrialist from Winterthur, no longer in the first flush of youth, suffers from chest pain and anxiety on the fourth day of her stay, presumably caused by the bracing climate in the high altitude of the valley — something that had never happened to her before.

The ladies' friend was always on the spot. He consoled, held hands, whispered encouragingly, accompanied ladies, supporting them to the spa if they were limping, spent whole afternoons having tea with lonely widows and chauffeured wire-haired dachshunds suffering from tummy ache to the vet in the village.

'He does not seem to be here this time', we said to each other after dinner on the second evening. Nor did we spot anyone hobbling in with a fresh plaster cast, nobody in mourning, no sign of a wire-haired dachshund whose coat had lost all its lustre.

The manager came to our table to greet us.

'How are you?'

'Good, as always, thank you.'

'The ladies' friend has failed to materialise this year.'

'The ladies' friend? Ahh, the soul-comforter. I call him the "soul comforter".'

'Good name. He appears not to be here.'

'No. He can't. You haven't heard?'

'What do you mean?'

The manager sat down with us, something he does not even do with longstanding guests.

'Right. As you are aware, he always consoled the unlucky ones among us, particularly the women. Actually, exclusively the female guests. And there is, in a house like this one, always a female in need of solace. He was first-class in this respect. Do you remember the story with the wire-haired dachshund? The lady wanted to depart at once, under protest, and send her lawyer. The ladies' friend, as you call him — his name, by the way, is Huber, plain Huber, though one would expect something a lot more exquisite —

made sure that the owner of the wire-haired dachshund stayed, and in the end went home so content and reconciled that she booked an additional week for the following season.

He was unsurpassed as a consoler of souls. I was often glad he existed and once offered to have him to stay for free. He rejected this vigorously, truly indignant, as if I had made an immoral proposal.

'And this year, he is not here.'

'That has nothing to do with it. It's a different story. Last year, shortly after you had been here, we had a death. The daughter of an old lady, not that young anymore herself, suffocated on a down-filled pillow in her bed. You cannot imagine how unpleasant this was for us. The mother broke down, the doctor gave injections, but they helped little. Only when the ladies' friend attended to the old lady, were our minds at rest. He arranged everything for the funeral. He went to the shops with her to buy mourning clothes. He drafted the death notice, took it to the printers and wrote out the addresses. He received the vicar, as well as the people from the police.

A week later, the funeral took place and we were amazed at how brave the old woman was. The ladies' friend led her by the arm. He supported her, as she stood at her daughter's grave. He sat next to her in the church and passed her his handkerchief.

In the evening after the funeral, the police came and arrested him. The colourful little piece of cloth that he always wore in his breast pocket had fallen out when he had leant over the bed and pushed the pillow down over her face. As he owned so many, he had not missed the one.'

131

'The broken legs, the anxiety attacks, the deaths of dachshunds in other years: that was all his work?'

'This can be assumed, even though there is no proof.'

'A very skilled director of accidents. And to what end?'

'In order to create an opportunity to console.'

'Did he at least allow the ladies to pay for his stay here?'

'No, he didn't need that. He is well off.'

'And what happened to him?'

'He has been convicted and is doing time.'

'In that case, he cannot comfort his last victim.'

'Oh yes, he can. The old lady, I heard, visits him every week in prison and the two intend to move in together as soon as he is out.'

The much desired son

They sat in the foyer after dinner, as they did every evening. Arthur read the paper, Marianne one of her fat novels. She did not read very attentively, but allowed herself to be distracted by the people walking past. She nodded in a friendly way to a lady here and a gentleman there. She knew most of them, at least by sight. For years, she and Arthur had been coming here for ten days every February.

In the back of the dining room, in their usual place, there was 'the family', as Arthur and Marianne called them. A real family as one would wish to have; mother, father, three children — a son and two daughters, and the grandfather. Well-off people, that was obvious, particularly from the woman's many silk outfits. The astonishing fact about the family was that the three children continued to come every year, too, though they were now no longer of an age when children go on holiday with their parents. The two girls were about twenty, the boy roughly seventeen.

'There you see the effect of a good upbringing', Marianne said, as she observed the family, particularly the son, with some satisfaction. When she talked about him to Arthur, she called him 'the son', and Arthur knew who was meant.

She never tired of looking at the son. Admittedly, he was indeed pleasant to look at, as even Arthur had to confess. Not particularly tall, but perfectly proportioned, neither too fat nor too slim. His dark hair was cut fashionably, with a parting, but not like a dandy. He wore glasses and they gave his face a slightly reserved look. In the evening, he always wore a dark suit with a light-coloured shirt and tie.

Where could one still find a young man who wore a tie? His shoes were Italian and the colour of the socks matched. 'A joy for the eyes', Marianne used to say.

This time, the older daughter had been joined by her boyfriend. She said goodnight early that evening and went upstairs with him.

'Two rooms or one?' Arthur asked himself and gazed after them. He thought that, in his time, when Marianne and he were young, it was not customary for engaged couples to share a room in a posh hotel. But in those days, they did not go on holiday in a hotel like this. One could not afford it. The young couple disappeared in the lift. But it was, of course, possible that they were already married, in any case.

Marianne had not paid any attention to them. She was reading her book. However, when a short time afterwards the son walked past, in order to call the waiter, she raised her head.

'One should have such a son', she sighed in a low voice and dreamily, more to herself than to Arthur. He did not respond.

Their childlessness appeared to have made her unhappy recently. They were by now both around sixty. Neither had wished to have children, nor had they wished to be childless. Unlike many other couples, they had not run from one doctor to another because of this. Indeed, Marianne had talked about her hairdresser, who had undergone two fertility operations, in a tone of slight amusement and definite disapproval: 'Despite all this, it's still not working.'

For her, it had never been an issue which of the two had been the cause of their childlessness. Nor had they delved into the relevant literature. Arthur had read somewhere, though, that in about half of the cases, the 'guilt' was with the man, if one could talk about guilt, of course. He believed this an astonishingly just and satisfactory arrangement on the part of nature.

He assumed that it had something to do with Marianne's age when she now, more often than in the past, hinted that she regretted not having any children. It did not matter to him, and he had the suspicion that it was a sign of his selfishness. Or was it only the thought, the shadow of disappointment, which he saw floating above his own life as above that of most of his contemporaries, that he did not want to pass on to a future generation? No, he would not have called himself depressive, and the shadow was definitely bearable, like a cloud darkening the sky temporarily on a sunny day.

Now, the son returned. Marianne barely managed to avert her eyes. He wore a yellow jumper under the blue blazer and his face was tanned from the winter sun. He really did look magnificent. Arthur waited for her to whisper the same sentence once again. That she thought it, he could tell from looking at her.

They finished their decaffeinated coffee, got up and went to the lift, nodding to the left and right and wishing everyone goodnight. While Marianne pressed the button, Arthur picked up the room key from the reception. The night porter, who always tilted his head a bit and looked at everyone from below, was already on duty and politely bid him goodnight. Miss Isabella, the hotel secretary, was no longer there.

135

Miss Isabella, so Arthur thought, was one of the high points of the hotel. Young and beautiful, she seemed enveloped in a natural purity that mesmerised him. A pity that she had already gone. He would have loved to say goodnight to her, too.

They went to their room. After he had closed the door behind them, Marianne cuddled up to him. She put her arms around his neck, kissed him and said: 'I wished we had a son like the son. It's not fair.'

'Think of the worries he'd cause us.'

'Ours wouldn't cause us any worries. As little as the son causes worries.'

'How can you know that?'

'That's obvious.'

Over the next few days, Marianne did not say anything like that again. Arthur observed her anxiously, worried that she might be depressed. But he was relieved to realise that nothing was wrong with her. On the contrary. She was full of joy about the dark blue sky, was sometimes downright boisterous, and they went on extended cross-country tours together over the frozen Engadin lakes.

Arthur believed, though, that he was noticing something else and he was fairly certain that he was right in his suspicion. The son tried to start a fling with Miss Isabella. Every time Arthur went to the reception to hang up the room key, or to check on his mail, or to buy a postage stamp — Arthur often found a reason to go to the reception during the course of a day — the son was there, leaning casually on the counter and asking Miss Isabella about some nonsense or other, or he simply flirted with her in the most blatant way.

Arthur reckoned that she was embarrassed. And when he fetched the key one night after dinner, but before they had their caffeine-free coffee in the foyer, the chap was there yet again, and Arthur had to observe how he grabbed Isabella under her chin, raised her head and forced her to look into his eyes.

He busied himself at the post rack, although he knew that he had already picked everything up, but he hoped that his presence would chase away the young man. It was no use. The son kept whispering to Isabella in the most intrusive way. In the end, Arthur had to beat a retreat, partly also because he feared losing control over himself.

While he and his wife were waiting for their coffee, the son walked past them, ears red, as Arthur noticed, to sit down with his family at the back.

'Bastard', Arthur thought furiously. And just as he had this thought, Marianne whispered again: 'Oh, to have such a son. . .' She said it very quietly.

'Stop this rubbish. You don't know what you're saying', he snarled at her, much too loudly, so that she asked him what was annoying him.

Arthur kept his discovery secret from Marianne. He did not want the son's teenage flirtations to be a permanent topic of their days in the Engadin. And he was, in fact, not sure what Marianne would make of the story. She would find it interesting, possibly be unfairly critical of Miss Isabella.

Like this: 'Just look at this floozy! Hopes to get herself a rich husband, and comes on to this naïve youngster so shamelessly.'

No, he would not be able to bear this. It was hard enough to have to watch how smitten the lout was with Isabella and how impertinently he behaved. Typical spoilt upper-class kid; probably thought all girls in the world were only there for him to have his way with them.

After that evening, Arthur began to watch developments systematically. Nearly every night he went into the village again, without Marianne, for a so-called digestive stroll, under all sorts of pretences. Oddly, Marianne did not even object that they sometimes went their separate ways during the day. She suddenly complained that her ankles ached, that she must have overexerted herself on the long tour into the Lower Engadin, and preferred sitting in the sun on a deckchair in front of the house.

That suited Arthur well. He did not have to find an excuse for each of his excursions. He could, for example, spend half an afternoon on the terrace of the restaurant near the ice rink and, torn between anger and jealousy, watch how the son encircled and beguiled Isabella without leaving her alone for a minute. To make it worse, he skated like a demi-god. Mind you, Isabella skated like a shining goddess. As they skated in serpentine lines towards each other, separated, and came together again, people turned towards them, and a woman who sat near Arthur on the terrace and ate Black Forest gateau said with a deep sigh to her friend: 'One ought to be able to skate like this.'

Isabella was obviously happy to skate with a good partner. She laughed loudly, which stabbed Arthur through the heart.

He would have loved to wait for her, put his arm around her shoulders like a father with the words: 'Don't let this young man impress you. There is nothing to him, surely; he is still wet behind the ears. Isabella, believe me, I am your friend. I really mean well. And as a friend I advise you, indeed, instruct you: hands off this young man — I mean — this boy. His family fortune should not blind you. Please, Isabella, for my sake.'

But he returned home without Isabella and when she was at the reception again in the evening, with her face slightly red, he did not say anything, of course, although the son was, for once, not there.

Marianne, incidentally, was not lying outside in a deck chair when he came back, nor was she waiting for him in one of the claret-coloured plush chairs in the foyer, and she was not in their room either. She had suddenly remembered that she needed to wash her cross-country outfit, but did not have any detergent. So she went shopping in the village.

Arthur was shocked. He hoped she had not seen him sitting on the terrace and staring in the direction of the ice rink. But she did not say a word about that, only: 'I think I saw the son ice skate with the floozy from the reception.'

'Surely, that's impossible', was the only response he could think of. Despite his fears, nothing more was said after Marianne's one sentence, and she did not refer to it again during the evening, although she cast such adoring looks towards the son, when he passed their table, that Arthur thought everyone would notice.

On another occasion, Arthur followed Isabella and the son all the way to the Fextal. They were without skis, as was he.

When he — a hundred metres behind them and always careful not to catch up — had to watch how the young man grabbed Isabella's hand, he implored the mountains to fall down, or at least to send a massive avalanche into the valley.

No avalanche came, however, and the mountains stood, uninterested and daft, while Arthur, heart bleeding, followed the couple all the way to the Restaurant Sonne, where they stopped off and where he could not follow them if he did not want to be recognised. So he trudged past the restaurant and the little church, and strode on bravely. He would have loved nothing better than to throw himself headfirst into the closest pile of snow and thrash around with his fists.

On the way back, he met Marianne. She said she could not just sit in front of the hotel, given the beautiful sunshine. They trotted back together, hand in hand. And after a short lie-down, they went down to dinner at half past seven. Before that, Arthur hung up the key at reception and took the opportunity to cast a punishing look at Isabella.

The story became increasingly conspicuous. One day, Arthur arrived on the scene just as the son leant over the counter towards Isabella and gave her a proper kiss on the mouth. And neither the son nor the girl seemed to mind that Arthur witnessed their gross behaviour. What, if he were to notify the management? He asked himself if that was not, in fact, his duty to do so, for Isabella's sake.

Then, however, he imagined the grinning face of the director. Only the day before, he had seen the looks with which this gentleman had followed a young girl. He could only wait. The jug goes to the well until it breaks, as the saying goes.

It broke on the night before Arthur's and Marianne's departure. They had remained in the dining room longer than usual. The hotel manager had joined them and treated them to a special bottle of wine.

'Are you aware that this is the tenth year you're on holiday with us?'

Arthur and Marianne had not thought of this. Back in their room, Arthur, who felt the effect of the quantity of wine he had drunk, said he wanted to stretch his legs. Marianne pretended that her feet hurt. Arthur got dressed. It was 11 o'clock.

He had no specific destination. He stomped through the snow drifts towards Sils. A bitterly cold wind blew from Maloja, the sky was clear and the full moon stood over the mountains, bright and wise. The night was light.

Shortly before the entrance to the village, Arthur turned around, not without having to fight a small personal disappointment. Had he expected to meet Isabella in the street at this time of night? That would have been a lucky coincidence, indeed. Why were there never any lucky coincidences, at least not for him?

Right next to the hotel, there was a stable for cattle, and in front of the gate there was always some straw. At that moment, Arthur saw something on the ground in the bright light of the moon. A hat. A light blue woollen cap with a tassel. A lady's hat. Arthur went to the stable and picked it up. It was Isabella's. He had watched her nearly every night as she pulled the light blue woollen cap with the big tassel over her hair when she went home.

Arthur held Isabella's hat in his hand. He suddenly felt hot. Then he heard a sound emerge from the stable. Not the noise of cows, more like a suppressed laugh. Arthur dropped the hat and carefully went around the corner, where there was a small window. He stood on his tiptoes and took a peek. From the other side, the brightness of the moon penetrated through a second window and lit up the backs and bums of the cows.

And then Arthur saw Isabella lie on a bedding of straw in the gangway of the stable, moonlight on her face and the rich, spoilt chap on top of her.

Arthur forgot to breathe. Blood shot into his head. Was the girl naked? The boy had pushed his trousers down to his knees.

Arthur heard steps behind him on the frozen snow. He saw how Marianne approached the stable from the direction of the hotel, stood still, listened and then disappeared around the other corner.

Arthur stepped out into the moonlight. He could not go back to the room right now. He did not want to force Marianne to explain herself, if she arrived after him. He let a good half hour pass and walked all the way back near the entrance of the village, before turning around. He did not run into a soul.

Nor was there anyone in the reception. The night porter was emptying the ashtrays in the foyer.

Marianne was already in bed. Snow clung to her shoes, which she had put down next to the door.

'You were away for a long time', she said.

'There is a glorious full moon outside', he retorted. Then they put plugs into their ears.

Thus, they did not hear the noise the cars made as they drove up an hour after Arthur's arrival, and they did not see the police get out. The farmer had looked into the stable again around half past midnight, because one of his cows was due to calve. On the straw bedding, which he had earlier put down for the calf, he discovered the bodies of a young man and the hotel secretary. Both had their heads bashed in. A piece of wood, smeared in blood, was next to them.

Arthur and Marianne were not aware of the murder until breakfast. They looked at each other. For Arthur, the matter was clear from the start: it had been Marianne. Dead for roughly an hour, the report of the forensic pathologist said. The timing would fit. Marianne had to have looked out of the window. Perhaps by chance, or might she possibly have witnessed the son and Isabella making a private arrangement? In any case, she looked out of the window when Arthur was out and she saw the son and Isabella disappear into the stable, immediately before he had found the girl's hat next to the stable door. Had Marianne seen him? He hoped not and did not think so either. Unless they had both play-acted fantastically well.

Marianne must then have run over to the stable. She looked through the window, broke into the stable like a furiously disappointed goddess of revenge, and battered Isabella and the son to death.

The police questioned everybody. They did not, however, manage to reach Marianne and Arthur.

Arthur was suddenly in a hurry. He did not want to stay until lunch. He paid the bill, dealing with Isabella's tear-stained colleague, packed the luggage into the car and attached the skis to the roof rack.

'Goodbye, see you next time. We're sorry about all of this. Have a good trip — 'til soon. Yes, of course, we'll book the same room for you again.'

They did not say a word until Silvaplana. And during the drive up the Julier Pass they did not talk either. Once, Arthur was tempted to drive the car over the edge. But the snow wall would have been too high.

One thing was clear: it would not be possible to continue living with Marianne. She had murdered Isabella. He pondered how he could kill Marianne. Why not lure her out of the car and push her down a ravine? Nobody could prove that it had not been an accident. Or suicide out of despair over the ghastly deed she had committed.

Once they had passed the summit, Marianne said quietly: 'There won't be a next time. I shall never come on holiday with you again. You have battered the two of them to death. You are a murderer.'

Arthur took a deep breath. This was the height of deviousness. She tried to frame him.

'Don't contradict me', Marianne said. 'I saw you near the stable. You have been following the girl for a long time. You thought I would not notice. I'll report you to the police.'

'I saw you, too', he wanted to say and shout to her face that she was a common murderer. But it was too late.

144

In front of them, across the road, there was a police car. Arthur had to stop. One of the policemen approached their car.

'Your papers.'

Arthur handed them to him. After the policeman had looked at them, he said: 'I have to arrest you. Both of you.'

Arthur did not ask why. They had to sit in the police car, Marianne in the front, Arthur in the back. They did the journey in reverse now, over the top of the pass and back down again towards the Engadin. They had just reached Silvaplana, when the police radio came on.

'Margna Two from Margna One. Over.'

'Margna One from Margna Two understood. Over.'

'Understood. Where are you? Over.'

'Understood. Entrance to Silvaplana. Over.'

'Understood. Have you got them? Over.'

'Understood. Yes, we bring them along. Over.'

'Understood. Treat them gently. We've just apprehended the culprit.'

'What? I thought —'

'Margna Two, please don't forget the radio rules. The two are no longer among the suspects. The night porter has confessed.'

'Understood. End.'

The driver hung up the microphone. The policeman in the back moved slightly away slightly from Arthur.

They did not need to conceal anything and reported everything they knew. The investigating judge thanked them personally.

'You have helped us greatly.'

The hotel manager offered them a room for another night free of charge, after they had finished testifying in the afternoon.

The night porter had committed the murder out of jealousy. He believed that Isabella had reciprocated his advances during the previous season and that she was now ignoring him because of a rich youngster.

Arthur and Marianne looked at each other.

'I think we should, perhaps, better drive home today, after all.'

The police had kindly brought their car to the hotel.

'All right then, see you next year', the hotel manager said.

'Next year', Arthur and Marianne responded with one voice.

Afterword

In the afterword to the enlarged 2004 German edition, I mused about readers' reactions to crime stories written by a theologian and, as this is still my main occupation, métier and, indeed, my calling, I want to come back to this theme.

Readers mostly laughed as they contemplated the seriousness of evil, but there was a definite hint that people should feel guilty at the thought of being entertained by nastiness. For me, the question arises whether this is not actually the essence of irony. What do you think?

Others expressed their displeasure that somebody would enjoy reading anything based on malice and nastiness. They reacted negatively to such wickedness: this clearly contravened cultural norms. Surely, if the world tries to turn itself into a better place, it ought to be made into a nicer reality. Some puzzled readers were rather confused and asked, 'How can a theologian write stories of this kind?' and this question was regularly followed by 'Should he not *ex officio* believe in the good in mankind?' — 'As if!' I say. 'It would be a poor vicar whose faith rested in the kindness of mankind instead of the benevolence of God.'

I wish to build on these thoughts about an expedition into the unknown territory that borders on narrative and theology and combines the two.

The Bible is full of stories. During my training, I learnt to read them as if they were a curtain that had to be pushed aside to reveal the real object, the theological system. I didn't like this. 'Why this game of hide-and-seek?' I asked both the Bible and Theology.

The theologian seemed to be disconcerted. How could anyone question something so self-evident? The Bible, on the other hand, was not going to be dissuaded from telling worldly, human tales. Tell the stories yourself and you'll see that it's not a game! When I first attempted to write something like a crime thriller, *Roma Termini* saw the light of day and was such a success that my then publishers asked for more manuscripts. Lo and behold, a few short stories penned during our annual holidays in the Engadin, were discovered hiding in my drawer.

Let me finish this note by proposing a toast to 'liberating laughter' and, with due reference to Luther, to merry sinfulness. Finally, I want to thank Sils Maria, with all its citizens and holiday guests: may they forgive me my mischievousness in writing these tales.

Ulrich Knellwolf
Zollikerberg, September 2019

By the way: the expedition into the lands of story-telling has taught me a lot; above all that we can only talk of the Bible's God by telling human stories.

Another book set in the same region of Switzerland — a family history describing two centuries of life in the high mountain valleys:

Marcella Maier
The Green Silk Shawl

Marcella Maier weaves the fascinating stories of her female ancestors on and around a green silk shawl that is handed down from mother to daughter.

This book is for everyone with an interest in the development of modern Europe and with the possibilities of oral history. Through the memories of successive generations of Swiss women, we relive Napoleon's marauding troops, early industrial action by washer women wanting better wages, the introduction of electricity (this 'work of the devil'), the beginnings of tourism and of a health service, as well as the deprivation brought by two world wars. The author's understated style brilliantly conveys the women's stoicism and their calm fortitude in the face of adversity: they sought solutions without complaint and just got on with their incredibly tough, but somehow affirming, lives.

www.thegreensilkshawl.co.uk

Lightning Source UK Ltd.
Milton Keynes UK
UKHW010626260120
357615UK00002B/92

9 780995 509337